The Lycanthrope Club: Book I

Story

Tristan Eifler

Editing

Lance Marcum

Brynn Huso

Kristan Overstreet

Artwork

Leonardo A. Vidal Fernandez

Dirk I. Tiede

Cover Art

Ashley Vanstone

Visit Daemoneye Publishing at http://daemoneye.net
Visit Lance's website at http://www.lancemarcum.com/
Visit Kristan's website at http://www.wlpcomics.com/ (some mature content)
Visit Leo's webcomic at http://www.alphaluna.net/
Visit Dirk's webcomic at http://www.paradigmshiftmanga.com/
Visit Ashley's website at http://ashkey.blogspot.com/

Published by Daemoneye Publishing

First edition November 2012
ISBN-13: 978-0-988-36891-0
ISBN-10: 0988368919

Prologue

The hunter stopped for a moment to catch his breath. He gazed nervously around the dense, mist-shrouded woods, his breath plainly visible in the cold morning air. Though he saw no sign of the creature he did not for a moment doubt it was still on his trail. His flight had carried him beyond his tribe's lands, through forest and over hill; still it pursued him. How he had evaded it for so long he did not know, but he was growing weary. He could not run forever.

He made a sharp left turn, ducking under a pine bough and leaping over the stump of a white ash. Thick undergrowth tore at his ankles as he ran, leaving long, red scratches across his skin. Driven by adrenaline and fear, he didn't even notice the pain. He risked a glance behind, and in doing so failed to notice that the timberline abruptly ended ahead. By the time he turned his head the ground before him had vanished. He screamed. His hand shot out instinctively and grabbed hold of a thick branch just before he felt gravity's tug.

The hunter dangled from the ledge. He peered down into the ravine. All he saw was a mist-filled grey void. Gritting his teeth, he tried to pull himself up the branch but failed. He was simply too tired. He glanced up at the grey, overcast sky and down at the gully below. His grip was weakening and he heard the wooden limb snapping. He shut his eyes, took a deep breath, and let go.

He fell.

The impact sent the hunter tumbling to his knees. He rose shakily, limbs aching, thick, black mud and dirty leaves clinging to his elbows, hands, and legs. Grimacing, he gazed around. Ahead he spied a small stream flanked by thin strips of sand and polished stones. The hunter scrambled over to the brook's edge, bent over and dipped his hands in the water, drinking the cold, clear liquid, splashing some on his face.

A howl pierced the air.

The hunter sprang to his feet. He scanned his surroundings, searching for some egress. The east wall – though not nearly as precipitous as the one he had dropped from – was made of loose, spongy earth that could not be easily scaled. Hesitating only a second longer, he started running along the gully.

The mist thickened as he ran. Aside from the sound of his moccasined feet and his pounding heart, all was silent. Minutes passed. The hunter's pace gradually slackened. His breaths grew shallow. Finally, he stumbled to the ground, panting.

Winded, he peered anxiously at the forest above. He scanned the ledge, searching for some way out of the gully. Seeing none, he walked over to the east side and clawed desperately at the dirt wall. Try as he might, he could not get a grip. In his mad scramble he slipped, falling headlong into the sludge. Groaning, the hunter slowly rose to his feet, spitting out a small brown glob. Wiping his hands, he looked around himself, and then froze.

A large object loomed ahead, its form partially obscured by the mist. The hunter took a few steps forward, narrowing his eyes. It looked like a pine tree that had fallen into the gully. Its tip was lodged the ground, leaving its base propped against the east wall. Thanking his good fortune, the hunter dashed over to the fallen pine and scrambled up its bulk. It was not an easy climb. The bark was slick from the mist and crumbled in his hands when he held it too tightly. Finally, he reached the top and carefully sidled off. He breathed a sigh of relief.

Then, there was a sound. At first the hunter did not know what it was – indeed, whether the sound was real or imagined. He stood perfectly still, and listened. A few tense seconds passed. A bead of sweat trickled down the hunter's forehead. Then, he heard it again. It was a deep, throaty rumble – not particularly loud, but the forest itself seemed to quiver in response.

The beast was here.

It had circled around, crossed the gully, and lain in wait for him.

Impotent rage filled the hunter. He shouted, waving furiously at the forest. He spat, cursed, and stomped the ground until exhaustion claimed him. He collapsed – conscious, but barely able to crawl, much less stand.

Then, melting seamlessly from the darkness like a shadow given substance, it appeared.

1

The thing was huge – vaguely lupine in shape, though it possessed certain disconcerting, un-wolflike qualities. Sheer size aside, the contours and proportions of its body did not confirm to lupine physiology. No ordinary wolf possessed such a wide frame, such a massive jaw or thick, shaggy coat. It was as though some dire spell had reached out across time and plucked it from era when such behemoths existed. Yet its archaic form was juxtaposed with a horrible *novelty*. It clearly had arms, not forelegs, though it still walked upon all fours. Its ears were long and pointed; its nose ended in a muzzle, yet there was a sort of vestigial chin above its neck. Its paws were wide, its digits long and doubly jointed, ending in wicked black claws.

The hunter weakly lifted his head. He rolled back onto his knees and tried to stand. His arms and legs trembled with effort, sweat and grime dripping from his skin. At last, he staggered to his feet. He peered ahead and saw that the beast was now less than twenty yards away. He slowly reached for a knife tucked in his belt. He took a deep breath, crouched low, and backed away, carefully circling away from the gully until his back was to the forest. The beast followed, neither closing nor widening the gap between them.

Seconds ticked by. Suddenly, the hunter felt a tug on his left leg. He yelped and glanced down. His foot had been caught in a tangle of briars. Cursing softly, he pulled himself out of the offending shrubbery. When he looked back up, the beast had stopped in its tracks. Confused by this, the hunter began stepping backwards, carefully watching the beast. The creature continued after him. The hunter narrowed his eyes. He stopped, and so did the beast. He tried the experiment again to the same result – when he stopped moving, so did it.

The creature was playing with him. It could have killed him any time it wanted, yet for whatever reason it had drawn out the chase for mile after mile.

The hunter's free hand curled into a shaking fist. Fear, frustration, fatigue and fury blurred into a single desperate impulse: to end it once and for all. He no longer cared if he lived or died, but he'd be damned if he let the thing toy with him any longer. He yelled at the beast, brandishing his knife in the air, daring it to come for him.

There was a deadly silence. Then the beast lifted its head into the air, bayed, and charged.

The hunter brought his knife to point with his foe. He pressed his free palm against the hilt, watching his nemesis. The beast moved through the forest like a juggernaut, trampling everything in its path. Closer and closer it grew, until-

There was a sound like a thousand branches snapping, followed by a hiss. The beast disappeared into the earth.

The hunter stood in stunned silence, mouth agape.

A deafening roar filled the forest. The hunter raised his blade but then quickly covered his ears, grimacing. The roar died down – replaced by long, plaintive howls, coming from where the beast had fallen.

Half-puzzled, half-frightened, the hunter lowered his hands. He slowly crept forward, weapon ready. He glanced at down where the beast had been and stopped dead in his tracks.

Whether it had formed naturally or been built and later abandoned, the pit had clearly been there for some time. The layer of branches, needles, loose soil, and other debris that once covered it had been so thick a sapling (which was now dangling from the edge) had taken root in it. The hunter had probably walked across it while retreating; only something as massive as the beast could have broken through.

The hunter carefully circled the hole. Dust from the sudden collapse of earth hung in the air. He knelt at the edge and carefully, cautiously, peered through the fallout into the gaping hole.

The beast lay sprawled on its back at the bottom of the pit, head lolled to one side. Its massive, black chest heaved up and down. Its yellow eyes were dim and weak. A faint, wet glimmer could be seen across its left arm and torso – blood, the hunter realized.

The hunter shook his head. It had shrugged off arrows, blades, hatchets and bullets. How could a short fall cause it such distress? Then, the hunter noticed something protruding from its left breast – a branch. It had snapped at such an angle to form a long, sharp point. The branch had gone straight through its torso, barely missing the spine.

Despite all the pain and suffering the beast had inflicted upon him and his people, the hunter could not help but admire its fortitude. A wound like that – by the hunter's reckoning – would have killed a grizzly bear. He sighed and sat down. It was over.

Time passed. The beast's howls of pain stopped, but its deep, hoarse breaths didn't. Every so often it would twitch or lift a trembling limb into the air. The hunter watched the beast with growing disquiet. Why wouldn't the thing die? Surely, no living thing, however strong, could survive such a devastating injury. Even if the branch hadn't punctured any organs the beast had lost so much blood that it was pooling around its body.

The beast whimpered. It was…pitiful. The hunter's heart betrayed a pang of sympathy. To leave it here in constant agony would be beyond cruel. Perhaps, he thought, he could climb down and cut the thing's throat, granting it release.

The hunter quickly dismissed the notion. He knew not what it was nor where it had come from but the beast had taken much from him. It did not deserve his mercy. Besides, even in its weakened state, it could still pose a threat.

The hunter stood, gave the beast one last look, turned, and walked away. The beast wailed in anguish as he left, its ululation filling the forest.

Chapter 1

Melinda Cooper stared dejectedly out the car window, watching the lush evergreen scenery roll by. She adjusted her glasses and glanced around her parents' van. Her father was sitting in the driver's seat, whistling a cheery tune. To his right her mother was slowly tracing a gloved finger along the crisscross of routes and roads depicted on a map, lips puckered in concentration. Melinda sighed and flopped back into her seat, blowing away a wisp of hair that obscured her left eye.

How had it come to this? She was going to spend the entirety of her spring break stuck out in the middle of nowhere. No electricity. No hot water. Bad food, sleeping bags, mosquitoes, and trees for toilets.

The whole thing had been her father's idea. Though her mother had initially balked at the idea of camping, he had ultimately convinced her that it would be A Good Learning Experience for Melinda. And once she was on his side there was no use arguing.

What made it worse was that her dad wanted to 'rough it.' After rummaging through the attic he had produced a set of camping equipment from his Eagle Scouts days, which included some old whittling knives, three army surplus sleeping bags, a set of cookware that was half rust, half metal and a tattered old cotton tent with so many holes in it that it resembled Swiss cheese. They had brought little else with them.

Melinda fumed. He could have at least brought that portable gas grill her uncle had given him for his birthday. Then they could have had real cooked food.

"Only twenty more minutes, honey," said Melinda's mother.

"Great!" exclaimed her father excitedly. He turned back to face Melinda with a grin. "You hear that, sport? Only twenty more minutes until we're at the campsite."

Melinda rolled her pale blue eyes. It really bugged her when her dad called her "sport."

"Shouldn't you be watching the road, dear?" said Melinda's mom, a hint of urgency in her voice.

Melinda's dad turned around and yelped.

"Sorry," he said with almost comical sheepishness as he swerved along a tight turn, missing the guard railing by mere inches.

Melinda sighed as she watched her father drive. No question about it, this was going to be hell. She glanced down at her backpack. At least they let her bring her books. Assuming her father didn't drag her on a hike every day, she might actually get some good reading time in.

"Melinda, darling," said her mother. "You haven't said a word since we left. Are you feeling all right?"

"Hmm," said Melinda.

"What was that?" said her mother.

"I said I'm OK," murmured Melinda slightly more audibly. She reached down, unzipped her backpack and pulled out a thick, worn paperback. Licking her thumb, she loosened her seat belt and flipped through the pages until she found her place.

"Melinda, you shouldn't read in the car," chided her mother, who had been watching her in the rear-view mirror.

Melinda rolled her eyes. "I'll be fine," she said, already on the second paragraph of the page.

"You'll get motion sickness, dear."

"I'm just trying to pass the time."

Melinda heard her mother sigh in what she considered an exaggerated, almost melodramatic manner.

"Alright, Melinda, don't say I didn't warn you."

"I'll be fine, *mother*," hissed Melinda through clenched teeth. "I'm just trying to pass the time."

"Aw, let her read," cut in her dad cheerfully. "Once we get to the campground we won't have any time for reading, eh?"

There was a long silence.

"What do you have planned for us anyway?" asked Melinda's mother.

"You name it," said Melinda's dad enthusiastically. "Hiking, fishing, rafting, hell, there's even an old quarry near the lake where we can go rock climbing. I threw the extra harness in the trunk just before we left."

"Oh, that sounds…exciting, dear," said Melinda's mom.

"You know I can't climb, dad," said Melinda. "I tried it once. Nearly broke my arm."

"You just bruised your elbow a bit, sport," said Melinda's dad. "And that was over a year ago. You've definitely put on some muscle since then."

"You really think so, dad?" said Melinda dryly.

"Sure! We'll take it easy. I'll find a really craggy spot with soft soil, get the harness nice and tight – it'll be safer than the rocknasium."

Melinda felt a sickening weight in the pit of her stomach. This was going to be hell.

* * *

The "campsite" proved to be a small clearing in the woods linked to the main road by a dusty dirt road barely wide enough for their vehicle. The ground was bare save for a few scattered beer cans and patches of yellowing grass. Melinda and her mother looked around, unimpressed. Melinda's dad, however, couldn't have been happier. He practically leaped out of the van and gazed about excitedly, reminding Melinda of a schoolboy home for the summer.

"Man, this is great!" he exclaimed, rubbing his hands. "I haven't been out here for years!" He turned back to the van, peering through the window. "Come on; let's break out the tent, the table…"

Groaning, Melinda pried herself out of the car, wobbling slightly as she stood. She steadied herself against the door. She stretched her thin, willowy body, running her hands over her hair. She squinted in the obtrusive afternoon light and dusty forest air. With a sigh she glanced over at her mother, who appeared to be just as fatigued as she was.

"Mom, remind me again why we're doing this?" whispered Melinda, first making certain her father wasn't in earshot.

"Because your father deserves a little vacation now and again, and this is how he likes to relax," replied her mother. "Besides, you needed to get out of the house."

"Then why couldn't we have gone on a trip that involves a hotel? With wireless internet, hot water, indoor bathrooms?"

"Look, honey," sighed Melinda's mother wearily. "Your father used to go camping all the time. He really loves it. He hasn't gone for a long time. Could you at least try to enjoy it for him? I'm making the effort."

Melinda sighed. "Well, yeah, I suppose I should. I love dad and everything, and I don't want to hurt his feelings, it's just…"

"Yes?"

"It's just…couldn't he have gone with some of his friends or something? Did he really have to take us with him? I was really looking forward to my spring break."

Her mother raised an eyebrow. "Oh really," she said smoothly. "And what were you planning to do for the next two-and-a-half weeks?"

"Well…I…" hesitated Melinda. "Maybe sit around, catch up on my reading."

"And how is that different from when you're at home?" said her mother. "Honestly, that's all you do - go to school, come home, go on the computer, read, and go to bed. I'm growing concerned about you, Melinda. It's a wonder you haven't started packing on weight."

"Mom!" hissed Melinda in protest.

"When was the last time you went outside for a walk, or rode a bike, or went to a friend's house for dinner or something?" continued her mother.

"What friends?" sighed Melinda. "You know all the girls at school hate me."

"That's not true."

"Yes it is," said Melinda glumly.

"What about Yvette?"

"Yvette?" Melinda hesitated, looking uncertain. "I…well, alright, *one* friend," she admitted.

"See?" said Melinda's mother pleasantly, stroking her daughter's hair. "If you made one I don't see why can't make more. You're really a very sweet, bright young woman."

"That's just the problem, mom," sighed Melinda, gently pushing her away. "I stand out. I'm a nerd. A geek. A freak. That's why Yvette and I get along – she's one too. I've given up trying to make more friends. Just the way things are."

Melinda's mother smiled.

"Well, they may have a point."

"MOM!"

"Kidding, kidding!" said Melinda's mother in a disarming voice. "I'm very proud that you're such an excellent student. I just, well…I just wish you would find some other interests. Like tennis, or…or ballet dancing or something. Or just…socialize. Go to a dance. Go out for a meal with someone from your school. Throw a wild party without telling us." She glanced over her shoulder at Melinda's father, who was lifting something very large and very heavy from the back of the van. She turned back to her daughter. "To tell the truth, the only reason that I went along with your father on this expedition was to expose you to some…alternative forms of recreation. Come on - give it a chance. For all you know you may love camping."

"Thanks, mom," snapped Melinda peevishly.

Melinda's mom sighed, rubbing her head. "I think the long ride here left you a bit…restless," she said diplomatically. "Why don't you start unpacking? I'll see if I convince your father to…to go on a solo hike to look around after we finish up. Give you a little time for yourself."

Melinda gave her a look, and then sighed.

The evening sun was setting over the hills, painting the western sky a fiery shade of orange. The air was alive with the myriad gentle noises of the forest - the buzz of the crickets, the caws of the crows, and the whisper of the wind as it blew through the pine needles.

The campsite now looked almost habitable. The empty beer cans lay crushed in a pile next to a tall evergreen. A triangular green tent stood around a roaring campfire surrounded by stones. Melinda's parents were sitting together on aluminum foldouts, watching the flickering flames.

Melinda's father turned to Melinda's mother.

"I told you this was a good idea," he said, smirking.

"Well, I have to admit this is much more enjoyable than I thought it'd be," said Melinda's mother happily. "I was afraid you were going to go Navy SEALs on us, but this is nice. Everything's so peaceful."

Several peaceful minutes passed. The couple continued to stare into the fire.

"Hey, where's Melinda?" said Melinda's father, glancing about the camp.

"She needed to use the restroom," said Melinda's mother. "She'll be back in a bit."

"Is it just me, or was Melinda…unhappy today?" asked Melinda's father hesitantly.

"It wasn't you," sighed Melinda's mother. "She's didn't want to come here, and she wasn't happy when I sided with you. Face it dear - she's just not an outdoors person."

"Eh. That's why I thought we ought to bring her out here. Toughen her up."

"In case you haven't noticed, dear, she's a girl, not a boy," laughed Melinda's mother, though something about the tone of her voice suggested she was only half joking.

"I know that," said Melinda's father, waving a hand dismissively. "But she spends all her time reading books…can't be good for her."

"When's the last time you read a book?" said Melinda's mother mischievously.

Melinda's father blushed.

"Look…I thought we agreed to expose her to a variety of different things. She can't live off books and computers alone."

"I'm more than aware of that," continued Melinda's mother evenly. "But if we force this on her she'll just shrink further into her shell. She has to be the one to make the decision, not us."

"So, what, we just let her sit in camp all day reading and then take her home?" said Melinda's father. "She's going to need a push."

"Maybe," said Melinda's mother, nodding. "But – and please, don't take this the wrong way – you do have a tendency to push too hard."

"Okay," he sighed. "I'll tell you what: If she's still miserable after three days we'll leave early, and I promise I won't bitch about it."

"Really dear, mind your language!" scolded Melinda's mother in jest. She leaned over and kissed him on the forehead.

Melinda was watching the sunset from a small hill a good distance from the campsite. She figured that if she was going to be knee-deep in nature she might as well see what the big fuss was over the panorama. It also meant precious time away from her parents. She watched the sun slowly dip beneath the distant horizon. Its dull orange radiance dimmed until there was nothing left but a thin sliver of light, and then, nothing. Melinda sighed, shook her head, and turned back to the camp.

"Don't see what the big deal is," she sighed. Her steps made soft crunching sounds against the thick forest floor as she walked. "Stupid forest, stupid camp, stupid, stupid, stupid," she muttered. "Should've just stayed at home…"

She kicked a pinecone.

"We get the camp set up, then he wants to go on a hike," she grumbled. "Then he wants to go fishing, THEN he wants to go rock climbing…Jesus. Take it down a notch."

A gentle breeze passed through the forest, sending leaves rustling across the ground. Melinda slowed to a stop, lowering her head.

"I mean, why can't they all leave me alone?" she said in a soft voice.

After a while, Melinda sighed wearily and continued onward.

The dim orange glow in the sky slowly faded as she walked. The shadows grew deeper. Melinda looked around uneasily. It was already so dark that she couldn't distinguish the path from the forest floor. She quickened her pace. The tempo of her footsteps gradually increased until it was a steady trot. Somewhere, an owl hooted.

She stopped, looking around.

"Hang on," she muttered to herself. "There should have been…that wooden sign by now."

Melinda backtracked a couple hundred yards.

"No, no, I must have passed it," she said uncertainly.

Melinda continued onward for a while. The air grew colder. Overhead, stars started to appear. Suddenly, she felt something sharp tear at her leg. Yelping, Melinda stumbled forward, nearly falling to her knees. She steadied herself and glared downward. There was some kind of bush, bramble patch or pile of fallen branches in her way.

"Damn it," she muttered.

Annoyance turned to alarm as she realized she had gone off the trail. Worse, she had no idea where she was. She gazed through the forest and up at distant hills, searching for some familiar landmark or light source. She saw nothing but trees and darkness.

Melinda considered her options. She could try calling out for help. There wasn't much noise out in the park so her voice might carry all the way back to the campsite.

Then, she was struck by a rebellious impulse. She could find her own damn way back to camp. If she got lost along the way it was her parents' fault for bringing her out here in the first place! Frustrated, angry, and tired, she marched deeper into the woods.

Her temper slowly dissipated as she wandered deeper into the park, replaced by fear. It was getting darker. She was lost, tired, and her feet hurt like hell. Swallowing her pride, she cupped her mouth and cried out at the top of her lungs.

"Hello?"

No response.

"Hello! Is anyone out there? I need help!"

Silence.

"Please! Anyone? Is anyone there?"

Silence.

"Anyone? Please, I'm lost! Anyone? ANYONE?"

Melinda leaned against a towering pine tree, gasping for air. She had absolutely no idea what to do. Should she keep going? Should she stay in one place? Should she try to build a fire? For that matter, how could she build a fire? She lowered her head and moaned, punching her fist against the base of the tree only to withdraw it with a cry of pain after making contact with the hard, gnarled bark.

It'll be okay, she reassured herself. *It's not that big a park, after all. There aren't supposed to be any dangerous animals. There's bound to be a ranger or two out there. They'll rescue me tomorrow - if not before the end of the night. Yeah.*

…Yet there was still a nagging uncertainty – an unsettling but undeniable possibility that she could be in real danger. She had never experienced anything like this in her entire life.

A thought crossed her mind. Her eyes were no good out here, but what about her ears? Maybe if she just stood really still she would pick up some sound from her campsite – or any campsite for that matter.

Melinda took a deep breath, shut her eyes, and listened. The sounds of the forest slowly filled her ears – the steady chirp of the crickets, the rustle of the wind blowing through the trees, faint, murmuring hoots of distant owls.

Eventually, Melinda opened her eyes and sighed. No good.

Another idea occurred to her. If she could get to a high enough vantage point she might be able to see the campfires or even the buildings near the visitors' center.

Melinda started walking again, searching for some hint of a slope or rise in the ground. It wasn't easy. Her eyesight had never been that good even with glasses and it was hard to distinguish anything in the darkness.

Then, she made out a rocky outcrop ahead. Her heart leapt.

Melinda hurried over to the base of the mound. Taking a deep breath, she hoisted herself up onto a waist-high boulder then hesitantly reached for the flattened top of another rock farther up. Shuddering as her soft palms gripped its cold, gritty surface, she flexed her arms, trying to lift herself up. Unfortunately, she couldn't hold on to its smooth-worn rounded edge and slid down. After a few more failed attempts she let go and stood there bent over, clutching her knees, panting.

Wait…what did dad say to do when climbing something like this? she thought.

Melinda ran her hands along the pitted exterior of the boulder. After a minute or so she felt a horizontal crack near its top. She jammed both hands into it, pressed her body against the rock, and lifted herself up. Arms trembling, she slowly raised her right leg, pushing her toes against the boulder for leverage. Grinding her teeth, Melinda slowly extended her right arm, trying to catch the edge of the top with her elbow. Then, her toes slipped and she fell, hitting the hard granite surface.

Groaning, she staggered to her feet. Melinda stepped off the boulder and walked away.

She wandered through the forest in a sort of daze. Several times she walked into a bush, fallen log, or other obstacle and was forced to go around.

Though she did not see it, a deep ravine lay ahead of her. Closer and closer she grew to the chasm…

She barely had time to scream as the ground collapsed beneath her.

* * *

"MELINDA!"

Melinda's mother's cry went unanswered. She stared into the darkness of the forest, anxiously rubbing her palms together. Her lips were tight with concern. Suddenly, she heard someone approaching from behind. She turned around and saw Melinda's father carrying a powerful flashlight in his right hand. The shadows around him swayed and stretched eerily as the torch's beam swung up and down. There was a frown etched upon his normally cheerful face.

"I checked all around the campsite," he said in a businesslike manner. "No sign of her."

"How long has it been?" asked Melinda's mother in a shaky voice.

Melinda's father looked down at his watch.

"About an hour," he said.

"Where could she have gotten off to?" she murmured, rubbing her forehead.

"Well, the last time I saw her she was heading towards the portable toilets near the main road. It isn't too far, but considering how dark it is I suppose she could've gotten lost. I told her to take a flashlight."

"Oh Lord," whispered Melinda's mother.

"Don't worry," said Melinda's father reassuringly. "There are other campsites out there and plenty of people still have fires going. I'm sure she'll stumble on one of them and find her way back."

"I don't know, I mean, we camped on the very edge of the park. What if she wandered into the woods?"

"I'm...pretty sure it won't happen. I mean...it's a fifty-fifty chance, right?"

* * *

It took a couple of seconds for Melinda to register the fact she had survived.

She shifted her body, wincing. Her back hurt like hell. Not only had it absorbed most of the impact of the fall but forest debris had slid up her shirt on the way down, cutting her into skin.

Melinda tried to stand but realized she was half-buried in what she could only assume was dirt, leaves, and fallen branches. It was pitch black – not even a hint of starlight. She reached out, feeling the rough, disconcertingly moist texture of the fallen earth around her. Suddenly, something slimy slithered across her left wrist. Melinda screamed, flailing her arms wildly in the air. She slumped back, sobbing softly.

A strange sound filled the air.

Slowly, Melinda raised her head. It was a rough, gravelly, erratic sound – like water slowly being sucked down a clogged drain. It wasn't something you'd expect to hear out in the forest.

Then, two dull red lights flared into existence before her.

Melinda stared at them in bewilderment. When she realized what they were, her very soul shrieked.

Eyes.

She could now perceive a massive, dark shape behind the eyes. And it was moving.

The creature lunged forward, rising from the muck and grime like a demon emerging from hell, a deep, inhuman snarl emanating from its throat. It reached out with an arm as thick as a young tree and grabbed her by the shoulder. Its grip was like a steel vice.

Melinda cried out in pain as she felt its immense weight press against her body, its fetid breath blowing across her face.

There was nowhere to run, nowhere to hide. Trembling, she shut her eyes, tears rolling down her cheeks, waiting for it to finish her.

The creature sunk its teeth into her shoulder. She screamed.

Then, it released her.

Melinda later swore the thing shuddered as though it had been struck. There was a whining sound. Then, she felt the creature slide down her body and sunk into the earth.

Still shaking with fear, Melinda opened an eye and peered down. She couldn't see a thing – not even the creature's eyes. The only thing she heard was the pounding of her heart. She felt around with her foot and almost immediately felt it brush up against something heavy and furry. She retracted her foot with a frightened scream. She waited for a minute, clutching her wounded side. Then two. The creature did not rise or even stir.

Still wary, Melinda began pulling her body out of the dirt. It was a slow, nerve-wracking process. Every time a branch or clod of dirt fell to the ground she froze and stared down at the creature, seeing if it had reacted. It didn't even twitch.

The terror of the encounter coupled with her escape from the pitfall caused something inside her to snap. With a strangled cry she turned and started scrambling up towards the surface, frantically clawing at dirt, roots and rock. It was, in every sense of the phrase, an uphill battle. The grade was steep and the soil was loose, offering little traction. At one point she slid down the pit and actually collided with the creature's unmoving form. The pain from the bite on her shoulder didn't help. Eventually, she got a solid grip on a long root system and managed to pull herself to the top. Gritting her teeth, she pushed up against the thin layer of soil and leaves above and emerged from the ground, blinking in the moonlight. She lifted herself up to the surface and ran off into the night.

* * *

Back in the pit, the remains of the creature were disintegrating. Fur fell from its body. Its hide blackened and flaked away like rotted parchment. Its muscles and organs atrophied into wizened, dry husks of dead tissue. Its skeleton was briefly visible before it too succumbed and crumbled into nothing. There was a sound that no one heard – a whimper of release. Then, there was silence.

* * *

Melinda's father sighed as he put the cell phone back in his pocket. He looked over at his wife, who was sitting next to the dying embers of the campfire, hands on her face.

"Well, it's a good thing you convinced me to take that thing along," he laughed nervously.

Melinda's mother looked up and gave him a cold, hard stare. "Yes, yes it is, and I wish you would take this a little more seriously," she said angrily.

"Oh come on, she'll be okay," he protested. "The rangers said that they could search the entire park in a day or two. I'll bet you she'll be with us before tomorrow night." He frowned. "Although I have to admit, this isn't like her. Why would she run off?"

"Maybe she didn't," responded Melinda's mother dismally.

"What, what, WHAT?" cried Melinda's father suddenly. "What do you want me to say, huh?"

Melinda's mother just stared silently back.

Melinda's father sighed. "At this point we really can't do anything about it. The rangers can't start the search until morning and it's too damn dark to leave the park. If she has any sense she'll stay put somewhere conspicuous."

Melinda's mother was silent.

"I'm going to bed," he muttered, and stalked off towards the tent.

Melinda's mother sat up and paced the campground nervously, occasionally glancing into the forest. With a defeated, worried moan she turned towards the tent.

Then she saw her.

"Melinda!" she cried joyously.

Melinda nodded dumbly as she staggered into the clearing. She looked as though she had been trampled by an angry mob. Her clothes were torn, her skin was caked with mud and leaves, and her hair was tangled and dirty. Her mother rushed towards her and gave her daughter a passionate hug. Her father peered through the tent flap, cried out in surprise and delight, and then leapt out to join them. The couple embraced their daughter, talking and laughing with relief.

"Honey! Honey! Thank God you're OK!"

"Where the heck have you been?"

"I mean, when you disappeared I was so worried!"

"We called the park rangers and everything! I'm so glad you're back!"

"Never do that again, do you hear me?"

"Do you need anything? Are you OK?"

Melinda cleared her throat.

"Uh, dad,"

"Yeah?"

"You're in your underwear."

"Oh, heh, yeah. Sorry," said Melinda's father, glancing downward.

"Honey…is that…blood?" said her mother, her voice suddenly filled with concern.

"Yeah," muttered Melinda. "I fell, but I'm better now…"

With that said, she collapsed into a heap.

* * *

Doctor Michaels whistled as she examined Melinda's forehead. "That must have been quite a nasty blow," she commented with a wan smile.

Melinda looked up at her from the examination table and shrugged.

"The strange thing is," continued Dr. Michaels, brushing aside some of Melinda's hair to get a better view of the wound. "There really hasn't been any significant damage. Blunt trauma to the head resulting in this kind of abrasion should've at least left a bruise or something, to say nothing of all the cuts on your back, but all I see are flesh wounds and fairly mild ones at that." The doctor stepped towards the sink and washed her gloved hands. "As for the bite on your shoulder, well, we'll get you checked for rabies. The way you described the encounter…not outside the realm of possibility."

Melinda's mother sat up from her plastic chair. "So, about that rabies test…" she said nervously.

"Oh, I already took a blood sample," sniffed the doctor. "However, it's better to err on the side of caution under these circumstances. We'll start treatment with human rabies immunoglobulin immediately and continue if the test comes up positive. Even if the animal was infected with rabies the survival rate is nearly 100% if you catch it right away, so you're in no danger."

Melinda's mother smiled.

"Thank you, doctor. Will she be ready for school next week?"

"Doubtless, if the young lady thinks she's ready," she responded.

Melinda sighed and nodded her head. "Yeah…actually, I'm really looking forward to getting back to the grind. I'm going to need a vacation after this vacation."

The doctor laughed. "All right, I think we're done here. Be sure to contact me if anything changes."

Melinda nodded.

Her mother turned to her as they exited the examining room. "So, you got your wish after all," she said, smiling wryly. "Half of it, at least."

"Yeah…" muttered Melinda. "I'm…really sorry about that."

"Sorry?" said her mother with surprise. "You got lost in the woods, fell into a pit, and nearly got mauled by a wild animal. I don't think you need to apologize for anything."

"But still," persisted Melinda. "I'm the one who got lost, and because of that dad lost his vacation. He probably won't get another chance to camp for half a year. Besides, I was…I was a bit of a brat on the trip."

Melinda's mother nodded. "You were," she said.

"MOM!"

"What?" she said innocently.

"You're not supposed to say that," she laughed.

"Well, I'm glad you noticed," chuckled her mother. "Just be sure apologize to your father as well - I think he'd appreciate it. But try not to blame yourself for what happened. We're just happy you're alive and well. Your father will get some more vacation time eventually."

"I'll go and do wherever and whatever he wants to this time," said Melinda. "Just as long as it doesn't involve camping."

* * *

Melinda's high school loomed before her like some grim temple dedicated to a pantheon of rather dull gods. The front was already crowded with students at varying levels of sleepiness slowly marching up to the main entrance, many squinting in the dim morning light. Behind her, bright yellow school buses and cars of nearly every make and model conceivable crowded the parking lot.

Sighing, Melinda trotted up the stairs, absently reading the words 'PINEBROOK HIGH SCHOOL' inscribed above in brass letters. She rubbed the side of her head. The bruise had completely vanished and it barely hurt at all now. It still bothered her, though. As long as it was there she couldn't forget about what had happened to her two weeks ago. It was an experience she'd gladly wipe from her memory.

She reached the wide double doors and entered the main hall, carefully slipping between two bulky football players. The two teens glanced at her as she passed them. One of them whispered something to the other and both started chuckling. Melinda ignored them, or at least tried. She made her way to her locker and started turning the dial on the lock. She opened the door, and then sighed. Someone had stuffed wet, wadded up tissue paper down her locker's vents again. It probably wasn't directed at her personally – it happened to nearly every student in the school sooner or later – but if anyone saw what had happened to her it would single her out. She carefully lifted one of her books and put it on top of the crumpled paper, obscuring it from sight. Satisfied that no one had noticed, she started selecting the textbooks she'd need for the next few classes.

Her nose twitched. The aroma of cloying perfume filled the air. Melinda immediately recognized the scent. She slowly turned around.

"So, whad'ya think of her new hairstyle?"

"Tch. Total tramp. She looks like some forty-year-old hooker now who hangs out at the bowling alley."

There they were – Cynthia Carpenter, Heidi Erickson, and Lily Forger - the three most popular, gorgeous, and uncompromisingly bitchy girls in the entire school. Melinda groaned. Alone, they were manageable, but together they could be downright sadistic. They particularly enjoyed singling out individual girls, spreading gossip about them and playing cruel pranks until their chosen victim was reduced to a teary wreck. It was sport for them.

Heidi was the tallest of the trio at 5'10." She was a vivacious redhead with curves that could kill. Her face was angular but made up for it by having a cute splattering of freckles, pouting red lips, and piercing emerald eyes. Her build was perfect - neither too flabby nor too skinny - though it wasn't really toned. Lily was a stunning Hispanic with bouncy curls of dark, shimmering brown hair. She was a bit on the heavy side but she carried the weight quite acceptably. She wore an extensive array of cosmetics, most notably a shimmering pink lipstick and dark blue eyeshade. As for Cynthia…she was one of those rare individuals who was effortlessly drop-dead beautiful. Stunning long blond hair, smooth, light pink skin, a gorgeous face with perfect complexion, and breasts that made every other girl in the school, Melinda included, green with envy - Cynthia had all this and more.

It looked like they were chatting with each other – talking about boys, the latest issue of Cosmopolitan, what they did on Saturday, and other such drivel. A few hangers-on hovered around the three girls. Melinda risked another glance and immediately regretted it. Cynthia had been looking in her direction and caught her eye. Smiling cruelly, the blonde started walking towards her. Sensing their leader had found a new target, Heidi and Lily followed, their predatory grins mirroring Cynthia's.

Melinda's heart sank. She turned around and started meaningfully riffling through her locker, knowing it would do her little good.

"Hello, girls!"

Melinda froze. She sighed, relieved, but did not relax entirely. She slowly turned around.

Yvette smiled brightly at the three girls, clutching an algebra textbook against her chest. Melinda saw Cynthia, Heidi, and Lily's eyes roll.

"Yeah, hi, Yvetta," said Cynthia wearily.

"It's Yvette, but it is kind of a strange name," said Yvette, a hint of a French accent in her voice.

"Whatever, Yvetta" said Heidi dismissively.

"So how was your Spring break," sneered Lily. "Find a new boyfriend over at the retirement home?"

"No," laughed Yvette. "A few of the employees are kind of cute, actually, but they're a little too old for me. You know, we could use some more volunteers down there, if you're looking for older men."

Melinda smiled slightly. From anyone else it would've sounded like a retort, but not from Yvette. She was just suggesting the trio of girls might find a new boyfriend among the volunteers at the retirement home.

"Thanks," interrupted Cynthia. "But we have better things to do on Saturday than give some senile old perv a sponge bath. Come on girls."

The three girls turned and melded into the crowd. Melinda regarded Yvette with an odd mixture of gratitude and frustration.

"Yvette, you do realize they hate your guts," said Melinda, shaking her head.

"They don't hate me, Melinda," said Yvette, somewhat resentfully.

"Well, maybe not hate," admitted Melinda. "But they don't respect you. They don't care about anyone besides themselves. Forget them."

"They're not that bad, Melinda," said Yvette, lowering her book to brush back her messy brown hair. "I know they seem like…"

"Bitches," supplied Melinda.

"…But they just put on that 'tough girl' image to stay popular," finished Yvette, ignoring this.

"They're not tough, Yvette," sighed Melinda. "I know how much you want to be friends with them again, but trust me; it's not going to happen. Unless your family becomes rich or you start dating the football team quarterback."

"It'll happen," replied Yvette. "It's just a test, see? I met all three of them in first grade when I first moved here. They were the only girls who would play with me then. They're really quite nice at heart."

Melinda gazed into Yvette's bright brown eyes and couldn't help but return her smile.

The bell rang.

"We'd better get to class," said Melinda, gesturing down the hall.

The two girls started walking side-by-side through the rapidly thinning crowd of students.

"So, how did your camping trip go?" asked Yvette pleasantly.

Melinda was silent for a moment.

"Let's just say I won't be going again any time soon," she said quietly.

Yvette frowned.

"Something wrong?"

Melinda bit her lower lip.

"Yeah," she said hoarsely. "I got lost in the woods, fell into a sinkhole and then this…this thing attacked me. This…animal. It was probably a wolf."

Yvette stopped in her tracks, staring at Melinda in shock.

"A wolf?"

"I…I think so."

"Wolves creep me out," said Yvette, shuddering. "Sounds horrible."

"Yeah, I could have been killed," said Melinda. "I'm still getting rabies shots. I should be alright, though. Just…don't go telling everyone what happened, okay?"

"Why?" said Yvette, puzzled.

"I'd just as soon forget all about it," said Melinda. "That, and I don't want to attract any attention. You know how some of the kids in this school can be. If you really have to hear the whole story we can talk about it at lunch."

"No….that's all right, Melinda," said Yvette, nodding. "I understand."

The pair walked a little farther, approaching one of the classrooms. The once bustling hallways were nearly empty now. Melinda reached for the doorknob and then stopped.

"There is…one more thing," said Melinda, staring down at her feet.

"Yes?"

"…I don't know," whispered Melinda. "Ever since I came back from the park…I dunno, I've felt kind of weird. I can't shake the feeling it's not over. The whole thing was just so…surreal."

Yvette placed a hand on Melinda's shoulder.

"It's just nerves," she said.

"It's not just nerves," responded Melinda sorely.

"You just had a near-death experience, Melinda," continued Yvette calmly. "It'll take some time for you to recover. Give it a couple of weeks. You should feel better by then."

Melinda slowly smiled, and then nodded.

Chapter 2

It had been two weeks since the ill-fated camping trip. Melinda's parents had left for a day-long company retreat, leaving her home alone.

Melinda lay in bed, asleep. The clock at her bedside read 12:58 AM. Her windows' blinds were shut, but a pale light shone through the thin gaps between the flaps, softly illuminating Melinda's face; her cheeks were blushed. She nodded uneasily on her crumpled pillow, alternately gripping and releasing her blanket. Suddenly, her eyes flashed open.

Groaning, she threw off the blanket, revealing her sweat-soaked body. She felt her forehead and winced. She had come down with a fever – a bad one. Melinda rose from her bed, desperately fanning herself. Her exertions only seemed to make it worse. Feeling nauseous, she slid off her bed and stumbled out into the hall.

She made her way to the bathroom, opened the door and stepped inside. Though there was a sky window in the ceiling the dim light from the stars and moon barely illuminated the room. She fumbled around for the light-switch, her hands gliding across the wall and smooth, cool marble of the sink counter. When the light flickered on everything went white. She yelped and shielded her eyes. She reached over and shut off the light and knelt to the floor of the bathroom, fighting the urge to vomit.

The heat gradually dissipated from her body, though the nausea persisted. With a groan, Melinda rose to her feet and glanced around. Her eyes, having adjusted to the present gloom, made out the familiar, albeit blurred, contours of her bathroom. She turned to the sink and turned on the faucet. She cupped her hands and splashed water on her face. The cool water helped soothe her strained body and nerves. Sighing, Melinda sat down on the floor and slowly lay back, gazing up at the sky window.

The full moon hung in the starry sky framed by the window, shining into the bathroom with a gentle alabaster glow. For some reason, Melinda found herself staring intently at the celestial orb. She had never seen the moon more clearly in all her life. Well, maybe she had… but she had never noticed how beautiful it was until now. She thought back to the camping trip when she had watched the sunset and began to understand how a natural phenomenon could invoke such wonder. She laid there on the frigid tile floor and bathed in the moonlight, a smile growing on her face.

A tingling sensation ran down Melinda's body - one so strong it made her shudder. Her temperature soared. Beads of perspiration trickled down her reddening skin. Melinda whimpered as the heat flowed down her arms and into her hands, intensifying at the end of her fingers, which turned bright red and swelled as though infected. They grew larger and larger until they resembled tiny grotesque balloons that were seconds away from exploding.

And explode they did.

With a blood-curdling crack all ten of her fingernails shattered before her eyes. Melinda swooned from the pain. She slowly opened her tear-filled eyes.

She had grown claws.

Large, curled, black claws – animal claws.

Both her hands began to stretch and bulge in impossible ways. Her fingers elongated and partially melded together at the joints. The skin of her palms thickened, becoming dark and tough - like the pads of paws. Melinda watched in horror, disgusted but unable to tear her gaze away from the metamorphosis she was undergoing.

A growing itch on her chest drew her attention away from her hands. Black, thick, curly hair had appeared between her petite breasts. The itching sensation - and the hair - slowly spread across her entire body. Melinda wanted desperately to scratch this irritation but she was afraid she'd shred herself.

Coupled with the fur and fever her body was now so hot that what little clothing she had on had become unbearable. Hesitating for a moment, she pulled off her shirt, threw it to the floor and then reached down and clumsily tore her panties off with her clawed hands. Now nude, she looked down at her body. The fur - yes, that's what it was, fur - already covered her head-to-toe.

What's happening to me? she thought, terrified.

Another wave of heat and pressure washed over her, this one far more intense and agonizing than before. A familiar pain erupted in her toes as ten more claws burst from her skin, shattering her nails. There was a hideous cracking sound as her knees bent forward while her heels migrated up her legs, shifting her weight onto the balls of her feet. Grimacing in pain, she rose up, steadying herself on the bathroom counter.

Then her arms and chest jerked wildly. making her lose her grip and fall back to the floor. The change was moving into her upper body! Her abs tightened, becoming hard as rocks. Her stomach compressed until it was as flat as an ironing board and then swelled with muscle. Her triceps twitched and grew several inches; her previously near-nonexistent biceps expanded to the size of grapefruits. Though partially obscured by her fur, her physique was rapidly beginning to resemble that of a bodybuilder.

Her heart beat faster and faster as the transformation ravaged her body. After what seemed an eternity the pressure finally abated. Melinda stumbled back to her feet, shaking her head in bewilderment. Then, just as she thought it was over, an intense pain erupted around her tailbone. Melinda gritted her teeth. It felt as though something sharp was trying to pierce her flesh from within. Shivering, she looked at the mirror, turning so her back faced it. A tiny nub pushed its way out just above her backside. It snaked outwards and sprouted fur, forming a black bushy tail. Melinda stared wide-eyed at it, mouth agape.

Melinda screamed as the veins in her neck and forehead throbbed uncontrollably. Her entire face cracked and slowly pushed outwards. She tasted the bitter tang of blood in her mouth as her teeth grew, becoming razor-sharp fangs. Her nose turned glossy black and swelled. Her expanding nose tingled. She inhaled deeply, smelling an astounding range of different odors all around her - some familiar, some wholly alien. Her ears traveled up along her temples, growing up and over her forehead forming two demonic points. The noises around her - her grunts, her moans, her breath, her heartbeat, the sound of her feet scraping across the tile floor pounded into her skull like the sound of giants. Melinda reeled back as sensory overload paralyzed her already overwhelmed mind.

The transformation accelerated. Her nose and jaw jutted out from her face in tandem, forming a short muzzle. Her glistening fangs lengthened, growing out of her blackening gums. Her eyes - once a dull azure - swirled and changed to a deep, feral yellow. Melinda screamed, her voice rapidly growing deeper and more guttural until it resembled the cry of a wild animal. Melinda took one final breath, and ROARED - all her pain, confusion, fear, and frustration exploding from her body like a supernova. Her world went hot, scorching white, and then slowly faded to darkness.

* * *

The first sensation she experienced when she awoke was a sickly sweet aroma.

Melinda's nose twitched, sniffing, taking in the air around it. She shuddered as numerous powerful scents - most of them revolting - reached her nostrils. Her eyes fluttered open and shut.

Everything felt so…weird. Her mind was awash with half-finished thoughts, desires, and sensations - half-dreaming, half-awake. She vaguely recalled something about fur and claws, but the notion soon drifted away. Slowly, her thoughts became more organized and lucid. Her body stirred. She tasted blood in her mouth. Then, awareness returned to her. Her yellow, wild eyes shot open, darting back and forth.

She was lying in her bathroom.

Melinda stumbled to her feet in a daze. She knew that something was wrong, but she couldn't remember what. Her memory was still hazy. Her eyes wandered over the sight of the bathroom sink, the soap bottle, the toilet, the mirror…

And there - staring back at her - was a black-furred, wolf-like creature standing on its hind legs.

Melinda screamed.

She immediately cupped her mouth.

Her voice - it was deeper.

She looked down at her hands. They were hairy paws adorned with razor-sharp talons.

No!

Melinda backed away in fear, slipping on the slick bathroom floor and landing on her butt. A sharp pain shot through her backside as she hit the ground. Yelping, she twisted her body around and stared down at her rear. She had bruised her tail.

Her tail?

She had a tail!

Melinda scrambled to her feet. It wasn't easy. Putting aside how slick the bathroom floor was she now stood on the balls of her feet rather than her heels. Finally, she managed to steady herself. Shivering in terror, she slowly looked back into the mirror. The wolf looked back at her.

She was it. She was the creature. A single word floated to the surface of her mind.

Werewolf.

"I'm…a *werewolf*," she whispered to herself.

Melinda stood there in shock. Her mind reeled in confusion and fear.

How was this possible? How did this happen? It had to be a dream.

…But it wasn't. Somehow, she knew with every fiber of her being that this was no illusion. She was a werewolf.

Lips quivering, Melinda stepped back into a corner of the room, crouched down to her knees, wrapped her arms around her legs, and shut her eyes. She just sat there huddling in the corner for well over a minute, deathly afraid.

Does…does this mean that I'll…I'll go nuts? Go on a rampage? she thought frantically.

Another minute passed. Nothing happened.

I…I feel different, thought Melinda anxiously. *But…I don't feel angry or anything. I just feel…different.*

It was difficult to put into words. Her mind was unused to her new form; it still thought she was human. Her bones, her muscles, her ears, her nose, her legs, and her arms all felt out of place. Yet these feelings of inconsistency were slowly fading away. It was as though some new "werewolf" part of her brain was taking over. The process wasn't invasive or frightening at all, though; it felt perfectly natural.

The most noticeable change was her skin. Being covered by fur was beyond mere words. She could feel it press against her legs as she rubbed them together. She could detect the slightest breeze in the air around her. It was strangely intoxicating. Next was her tail. It took her a while to locate the muscles controlling it and even longer to master them. Having a tail was incredibly strange. It felt particularly strange when she wagged while her body remained still. Her increased mass, while disorienting, made her feel more powerful and confident than she ever had before.

Hmmm…

Melinda's fear of herself waned. She rose to her feet - more smoothly this time - and stepped towards the mirror. Her toe claws made little clicking noises on the tile floor as she approached the counter. Once again she saw the black, female wolf creature staring at back at her. It was odd. All the monster movies always portrayed werewolves as hideous, drooling monstrosities of flesh and fur. She didn't look anything like that. She looked like, well…what you would get if you took the body of a human and the body of a wolf and melded them together; her canine and human characteristics complimented each other perfectly.

She was, in fact, beautiful.

The transformation had enhanced her build. Her skinny arms had been replaced by smooth, fur-covered bulks of toned muscle. Her chicken legs now looked powerful and taut. Her hips were smooth and round while her abs were as tight as a drum. She had grown - and Melinda gasped at this - to at least seven feet in height.

"Rrrwow!" breathed Melinda.

She blinked. Oh yeah, her voice - it had changed as well. She looked at herself in the mirror, and spoke.

"My name is Melinda," intoned the werewolf before her.

Melinda almost jumped this time. It still sounded like her, but her voice sounded much deeper - much stronger. It was kind of cool.

Now utterly fascinated by her new self, Melinda turned her attention to her face. Her head was decidedly more wolf-like than any other part of her body. It was covered in a short, fine layer of black fur that shone in the moonlight. Her nose and jaw formed a short, sleek muzzle. Her ears were now pointed tufts that twitched in the direction of the slightest sound. Despite all this it was clearly not the head of an animal. For one thing, her muzzle was not complete; the contours of her face were gentle and smooth. Her yellow eyes shone with intelligence and energy. Finally, the hair on her head had not been replaced by fur. As a matter of fact it had gotten longer. Her stubby bowl cut had been transformed into long, luxurious ebony locks. She sighed happily as she caressed her new mane.

"Maybe…maybe this won't be so bad," whispered Melinda.

She felt remarkably calm. She was, however, beginning to wonder what she was going to do next. Then, her stomach growled, providing her with an answer.

She was ravenously hungry.

* * *

Melinda carefully made her way down the stairs leading into the main hallway. Her clawed hands gripped the polished wood rail tightly as she descended; although she was beginning to master her new body's motor controls she didn't want to take any chances. Because the steps were so small relative to her feet she was forced to adopt a short, shuffling pace - a stride rather unsuited to her massive legs.

Clearly, staircases were not designed with werewolves in mind.

In truth it hardly bothered Melinda. She was far too busy exploring her enhanced sense of smell. She continuously sniffed the air in an almost a trance-like state - sampling an amazing buffet of scents and aromas. Some she had smelled before - soap, deodorant, bleach, apples, grass, and many more. Others were new to her but she instantly knew what they were - the musky smell of human sweat, the metallic-burning stench of electrical wires, and the cauldron of gut-churning odors wafting from the bathroom. Some were completely unidentifiable. Curiously, Melinda found that if she focused on a single scent it often broke into several parts. The smell of wood, for instance, had at least three "component" scents to it. It was absolutely incredible. She could have easily spent the entire evening just wandering around the house, smelling everything in sight.

Melinda looked around quizzically as she entered the downstairs hallway. There was something off about the lighting. She glanced up at the ceiling lamp at the base of the stairway. It didn't appear to be giving off any illumination at all. She checked the switch besides her, and realized the lamp was turned off. Given that it was the only source of light in the hall it should have been pitch-black.

Then, it hit her. She could see in the dark! Only in black and white and shades of gray, it seemed, but her vision was nearly perfect. She didn't need glasses anymore. Melinda chuckled happily, waving her left paw in front of her face.

Her sense of hearing had greatly improved as well. Her triangular ears were like two miniature radio dishes, twitching this way and that in response the softest of sounds. Melinda discovered that the average suburban home could be quite noisy at night to a keen enough ear. She could hear the buzz of the outdoor electrical lights, the sudden cracks and drones of the house settling, the constant rumble of the air conditioning, the water heater, the refrigerator…

The refrigerator…

Melinda rubbed her furry stomach. She was *really* hungry now.

The wolf-girl trotted into the kitchen, bent over and opened the refrigerator door. The room was softly illuminated by a white glow. Hundreds of new, appetizing smells assailed her. Melinda licked her chops in anticipation.

She scanned the various bottles, cans, boxes and foodstuffs arrayed before her. Her usual snack of choice was a grilled cheese sandwich on rye, but for some reason that didn't sound too appealing right now. What she really wanted was…meat – juicy, tender, mouth-watering meat. This was certainly a peculiar craving for her as she was practically a vegetarian, but she did not question her newfound hunger for a moment. She started with a packet of lunchmeat. She tore open the flimsy paper wrapper and swallowed the bundle of cold cut turkey in a single gulp. The instant the meat touched her tongue her entire mouth tingled. Overcome by sudden, desperate hunger Melinda savagely shoved aside a dozen or so bottles and reached deeper into the fridge. She ripped open a package of baloney with her fangs and devoured its contents. She then dove in even deeper - irately tossing aside anything that didn't have the slightest trace of meat in it. Bottles, cans, bags, and other associated items fell behind her, bursting open and splattering across the clean kitchen floor. She opened the bottom drawer of the refrigerator and found a raw tri-tip steak marinating in a pan of BBQ sauce - jackpot. She grabbed the tantalizing meal and took a massive bite out of it. Thick, red juice squirted from between her teeth as she chewed. Melinda smiled wickedly. She consumed the entire steak in two more bites.

She was still hungry.

Melinda turned to the pantry. She opened the door and peered inside, sniffing. She grabbed a bag of potato chips and some beef jerky off the shelf. She started with the jerky, her sharp teeth and powerful jaw making quick work of the chewy, seasoned meat. She then tore open the bag of chips and stuffed the crunchy things down her gullet. They didn't taste nearly as good but were filling.

Satisfied for the moment, Melinda stood up - shaking her long lupine head to throw off the bits of food that had fallen into her mane during her feast. She glanced back at the broken bottles and scattered food items behind her.

Oops, she thought. *Well, I was pretty hungry. I can clean it up later.*

Suddenly, she started chuckling. She still couldn't believe that this was really her, that she had actually become a werewolf. Sighing, she leaned up against the kitchen door, slowly rolling her neck and stretching her long, toned arms over her head. She stared down to admire her sleek, muscular body. She flexed her powerful biceps in an exaggerated, macho fashion, breaking into laughter soon after at the sheer silliness of it.

It was about then that she felt this… vigor growing inside her. It was a kind of extraordinary confidence – an unquestioning acceptance of her new form. The sensation was a little unsettling at first, but gradually Melinda grew to like it. All of her cares and worries slowly drifted away. She stepped out of the kitchen and into the dining room, which was adjacent to the backyard. When she caught sight of the full moon through the patio windows she froze mid-step. She stood at attention, utterly transfixed by the luminous white sphere.

*It's so beautiful…*thought Melinda dreamily.

She lifted her head up and howled softly.

Her paws immediately flew to her mouth.

Did I just do that? It felt so…normal, like a yawn.

After a moment's thought, she shrugged, smiling. She howled again, this time more freely and loudly.

As moonlight continued to shine down upon her she began to feel a little wild. She shivered and fell down to four feet, growling menacingly, reveling in her newfound strength. She glanced through the lower patio window and into the night. It was calling to her.

Wait…wait a minute…what am I doing? thought Melinda suddenly.

She shook her head as though trying to recover from a stupor. What were these new feelings? What was happening to her? Was this how it started? Was this the point where the victim of the curse lost control to the beast within? She didn't want that! And yet…

…And yet she didn't feel enraged or bloodthirsty and certainly didn't want to hurt anyone. She was just full of boundless energy. She wanted to get out of this stuffy house and run in the moonlight. She wanted to feel the dirt beneath her feet and the wind blowing through her fur. She wanted to hear the sounds of the forest and smell the sweet scent of pine trees. It seemed a waste - almost a travesty - to just stand around when there was a whole world out there just waiting to be explored. It was a yearning she could no longer deny.

But where could she go?

There was a wildlife preserve only three blocks away from her house. It would be the perfect place for her to spend the evening. The young wolf-girl opened the screen door and scampered out into the moonlit night.

* * *

Melinda had to cut through a few of her neighbors' backyards to get to the park. It was either that or run out onto the street. The risk of being caught was frightening yet strangely exhilarating. She was almost disappointed when she made it out of the neighborhood without so much of a light being turned on or a dog barking at her. When she finally arrived at the entrance to the wildlife preserve – a cul-de-sac with a small, open gate leading into the preserve – her heart soared with joy. Thousands of new and interesting scents wafted in the evening breeze. Her ears couldn't keep up with the endless multitude of sounds emanating from the forest. Shivering with excitement, Melinda ran through the gate and entered the preserve.

It was as if she had dived underwater. The forest milieu engulfed every one of her five senses. There were so many details, so many different smells, sights, and sounds - so alien and yet so familiar and welcome. Overwhelmed, Melinda did the first thing that came to her mind: she ran. At first it was a persistent two-legged jog, but as she traveled farther and farther into the woods she fell to all fours and broke into an all-out sprint. Towering evergreens, verdant bushes, and tall grass shot past her as she sped furiously through the forest.

Melinda had encountered great difficulty putting into words what she had experienced since becoming a werewolf, and was beginning to understand why this was so. No words could adequately describe it. Words were human things, and what she was experiencing was beyond human understanding. The only thing she knew for certain was that it felt absolutely glorious. She was no longer human, but neither was she a wolf - she was the best of both worlds.

By the time Melinda had to stop to rest she could have very well been in the next county. She slowed to a trot, panting - exhausted, hungry, but happy - her long red tongue lolling out the side of her mouth. She took a deep breath, savoring the crisp evening air. Suddenly, her keen, pointed ears perked up. They made out the telltale trickle of water not too far off. Feeling thirsty, Melinda wandered in the direction of the sound and was soon rewarded with the sight of a burbling brook. She bent over and started lapping at the surprisingly clear and refreshing water. She reached down with cupped paws and splashed some of the water into her face, licking her black glossy nose as quivering beads of water ran down her muzzle. Her thirst quenched, Melinda sighed and lay down on her stomach. She twirled a solitary talon in the brook, watching the ripples spread. Her distorted, wolfish reflection flickered on the mirror-like surface of the water.

How did this happen? wondered Melinda thoughtfully. *It seems utterly impossible…but here I am.*

She gazed up at the moon through the branches.

Maybe…maybe I've died and gone to heaven.

It didn't seem like such a wild supposition. Perhaps she had been killed in the park and was living out some long forgotten fantasy of hers in the afterlife. Who knew?

Mind still wandering, she thought back to the creature that had attacked her. Assuming she wasn't dead or in a coma, it must have been a werewolf as well. Were there more werewolves out there? Perhaps there was a hidden population of werewolves living all over the world. Would she ever meet another like her? There were just so many questions she wanted to ask.

Melinda was amazed at how relaxed she was. She rolled over onto her back and stared up at the starry sky with her deep yellow eyes. She traced a few familiar constellations with a long, talon-adorned finger.

The evening wind gently blew through the forest, causing the grass and branches of the trees to dance. A sharp aroma suddenly filled Melinda's nostrils. She looked up curiously, sniffing at the air. The smell was new to her, but somehow she knew what it was: a deer. Another strange feeling came over her then. Her body tensed up. She stood up on all fours and slunk into the undergrowth.

Following the scent she came upon a small, secluded clearing. Standing there - drinking peacefully from the sparkling waters of the brook from before - was a doe. The scene was so picturesque it seemed surreal.

Melinda shifted uneasily from paw to paw from her hiding spot in the bushes. Hearing the faint sound of leaves being upturned, the doe looked up. Melinda instinctively crouched to the dirt and froze. After a while it turned and dipped its head back into the stream. Melinda licked her lips nervously as she stared at the docile creature. It smelled…good.

The realization hit her like a slap in the face: she wanted to eat the doe!

Her human scruples immediately rebelled against this disturbing impulse. She couldn't kill a harmless animal for food! Anyways, how could she cook it out here? A raw steak may have been one thing, but a freshly killed deer was another.

To Melinda's astonishment a second voice inside her replied: She was getting hungry again and the deer was the only food for miles. Besides, there was nothing evil, cruel, or wasteful about eating the doe; all living things had to eat to survive. She may have once been human, but now she was also a wolf, and a wolf needed to hunt. It was in her nature.

Melinda was becoming morbidly fascinated by the idea. She wondered what a deer would taste like. If its scent were any indication of its flavor it would be absolutely delicious - much better than the sauce-soaked hunk of cold meat she had eaten hours ago. Also, Melinda was feeling a tremendous urge inside to chase the doe - to hunt. Her body crackled with pent-up energy. She inwardly knew that she had yet to use a fraction of her full strength and eagerly wanted to see just how powerful she had become.

As she sat there the deer suddenly looked up. It stared directly at Melinda with its probing black eyes. It turned around and fled into the surrounding woods in a flash. The sight of its retreating rump proved too much for Melinda. Overpowered by instinct, she burst from the bushes with a savage growl and chased after the fleeing doe.

The moment Melinda initiated the chase she felt as though she had been reborn. The thrill of the hunt was upon her. Her entire world consisted of only herself and her prey. She was the beast, the hunter, the line between life and death. She could sense the rhythms and cycles of the natural world around her - the trees, the animals, the sky, the stars - and she was a part of it. It was beyond anything Melinda had ever experienced. She felt as though she would explode from the sheer excitement of the moment.

The scenery around her blurred while the outline of the deer became crystal clear. Melinda found herself seemingly drifting in and out of consciousness. Then, a final surge of energy suffused her. She leapt into the air with a savage howl and tackled the creature to the ground. Her powerful jaws immediately locked onto its long, brown neck and squeezed. Blood filled her maw. The doe struggled madly in her grasp, but was unable to move an inch under the werewolf's massive weight.

Melinda could hear and feel its heartbeat as she held it in a deadly embrace. It slowed, becoming fainter and fainter, until it stopped with a shudder. Still brimming with adrenaline, Melinda did not relinquish her grip on its neck. She lay there beside the twitching body, panting, the bloody haze slowly fading from her vision. She looked down at the animal in her mouth.

It was dead.

A sobering wave of guilt rushed over Melinda. She spat out the doe and padded back as though afraid the creature would rise up and take its revenge. She looked down at her blood-soaked paws and whined.

No…no…no…

She stared at the fallen doe. It looked so pathetic and sad lying there. For the first time since she had left her house Melinda was afraid of what she had become. What would have happened if it had been a human out in the woods? Would she have hunted and killed him as well?

Her stomach growled.

Scared as she was, her hunger was getting unbearable. Melinda sighed dejectedly and walked over to the doe.

"I'm sorry I took your life," she said softly into its ears. "I will make sure your death does not go to waste."

She knelt down beside the body; it was still warm. She stared down at the creature's brown-furred flank.

She was supposed to eat this?

Grimacing, Melinda bent over licked the wound in the deer's neck. As her tongue caressed the bloody mess, a familiar tingling sensation shot through it and ran down her spine. Her long, black tail perked up and began to wag.

It was the best thing she had ever tasted.

Melinda tore into her meal, pausing once halfway through to howl at the moon.

* * *

Something sharp prodded Melinda's left shoulder. It was a tree branch.

Her eyes opened to meet the stinging radiance of the morning sun. Melinda groaned and rolled over onto her back, shivering. There was a chill in the air. Goosebumps peppered her skin. She looked around sleepily.

She was in the middle of a mist-filled forest huddled up against the base of a tree, completely naked. She lay there, staring blankly into space, until she remembered what had happened.

"Oh yeah, I changed into a werewolf," muttered Melinda to herself.

She glanced down and made out the familiar shape of her pale, pink, scrawny body. She raised her hands. They were soft, delicate, clawless appendages once again. The night was over and she was human. Strange…she was almost disappointed.

Then, the reality of the situation hit her like a sack of bricks. She was out in the middle of nowhere, tired, cold, and naked.

"Crap," breathed Melinda, rubbing her forehead.

Chapter 3

Melinda winced. She felt a wet sting on the bottom of her left foot. She lifted her leg, wobbling, waving her arms to maintain balance. She inverted the offending foot in the air and examined it. The forest floor had rendered her sole a filthy black but without her glasses she couldn't make out much detail. Sighing, she slowly lowered herself to the ground, crossed her legs, and peered down at the bottom of her injured foot. It looked as though a broken branch had cut into skin, leaving a nasty gash that was still bleeding. She glanced over at her other foot; it was little better off.

Melinda groaned. Nearly every other step she took inevitably resulted in some kind of puncture or scratch. It was like walking on a pile of thumbtacks. The morning chill was almost as bad - especially given that she was completely naked. The slightest breeze made her shiver.

Although she had never touched a drop of alcohol in her life, Melinda was beginning to appreciate what a hangover might feel like. The night before had been a wondrous, euphoric experience, but now it was over and after being suspended for so long reality had a tendency to fall back down - hard. She had stranded herself out in the woods. She had no idea where she was, indeed, whether or not she was still in the confines of the wildlife preserve. It would probably take a whole day's walking just to get within sight of civilization. That, however, wasn't her biggest concern. What really worried Melinda was exactly how she was going to explain this to her parents. Numerous, desperate explanations and excuses were already forming in her mind, but all of them ultimately involved her getting into compromising situations that would a) attract unwanted attention or b) just get her in trouble anyways: getting kidnapped, going to a party and getting drunk, and other, even more insalubrious activities. And that was assuming she could find her way home on her own. The thought of having to walk up to a complete stranger - naked as a jaybird - brought her to tears.

She staggered to her feet, hugging her shoulders to ward off the cold. She took a step forward.

Snap.

Melinda swore violently as she stumbled over yet another sharp obstacle. Her feet were really starting to hurt now and the cold was getting unbearable.

I could really go for that nice thick pelt of fur right about now, she thought. *Not to mention the padded feet... damn that hurts. If only I had had the sense to head home before the end of the night instead of sleeping out in the middle of the preserve!*

The last thing she remembered was lying down at the trunk of a tree, sluggish and lethargic from the heavy meal of venison. She must have dozed off there - lulled to sleep by the peaceful sounds of the forest.

Stupid, stupid, stupid!

Melinda stared off into the forest. She sighed.

Then, a thought occurred to her: If she could shift back to her wolf form now it just might be possible for her to beat her parents' home, thus avoiding having to explain to them why she had been found naked in the woods miles away from town.

She glanced up at the morning sun. It couldn't be any later than 9 o'clock, and her parents weren't due back until around ten. That gave her at least an hour - more than enough time for her werewolf form. Her enhanced sense of smell would guide her home; all she had to do was follow the stench of car exhaust.

It was all sounding good until she remembered that werewolves only transformed in the light of the full moon.

Melinda looked up suddenly.

…Or did they? Legends also described werewolves as mindless, hulking, bloodthirsty brutes that hungered for human flesh. They had certainly gotten that part wrong. If they had been mistaken about that… then maybe, just maybe they had been wrong about the role of the moon as well.

Granted, the moon had definitely been the catalyst of her initial transformation, but was moonlight actually necessary for her to change? It was certainly worth a shot. She had nothing to lose.

Melinda glanced around nervously. Although the chances of anyone seeing her in the forest were slim to none she still felt a degree of trepidation trying this out in the open. Finally, she shut her eyes and concentrated.

…How am I supposed to do this again?

First, she tried visualizing herself as a werewolf. She pictured herself with long, black fur, glowing yellow eyes, pointed ears, a muzzle, and a wagging tail. She imagined her frail arms and legs bulging up with flesh and sinew. She imagined her pale, delicate hands morphing into rough paws with delightfully sharp talons. She thought back to her image in the bathroom mirror just after she had transformed - that primordial epitome of feminine strength, form, and beauty - and how she had become that creature. Apart from a small tingle of delight as she recalled those virgin sensations, nothing happened.

Disappointed, Melinda opened her eyes and looked down at her skinny body. She flexed her arms and legs, willing them to change - willing them grow fur and gain muscle. Again, nothing happened.

This isn't going to work, she thought grimly.

She tried growling. She tried howling. She tried stretching. Nothing. Exhausted, Melinda knelt to the ground. She felt sharp forest debris press up against her bare knees and bottom.

Now what am I going to do? thought Melinda bitterly. *This…this sucks. I want to be a werewolf again!*

A tear trickled down her cheek. She sobbed despondently, screaming in frustration.

Then, her bloodshot eyes narrowed with resolve. There had to be a way. There just had to be something she had missed! She mentally replayed the whole night from beginning to end - the burning heat, the transformation, the woods, the moon…

A prickling sensation ran across her skin. She sat up suddenly, staring into the woods.

The moon was the key. The mere thought of it now made Melinda tingle with delight. She remembered what it was like to be a werewolf - to be in touch with the land, to be part of the land - to feel such wild power coursing through her body. It had been transcendent.

Then, a strange heat enveloped her. It grew in intensity until it felt as though she was sitting in an oven. Melinda's eyes widened.

Her head shot down towards her shaking hands. Her fingertips bulged and then burst, revealing long, sharp, black talons. Her palms hardened into thick leather pads. Black hair slowly sprouted from every inch of her body. Below, her feet and legs began to stretch and twist. Her muscles started to gain mass. Melinda shuddered and fell to her stomach as the transformation overwhelmed her. She gritted her elongating teeth, steeling herself for the agony to come.

But oddly enough, it didn't feel so bad this time. Even as the change progressed through what Melinda remembered as the most excruciating phases - the repositioning of her bones and the extension of her face to form her muzzle - the pain never exceeded that of a very uncomfortable stretch. It was proceeding more rapidly as well.

Melinda rolled over onto her back and spread her arms and legs. She felt her tail push its way out. The stubby black hair on her head grew out into the long, flowing black mane. Her chest heaved up and down as she drew in the morning air, gasping like a fish out of water, her eyes locked shut, a strained look on her lupine face. A final wave of heat and pressure washed over her. Melinda shook violently and howled into the morning sky, heralding her transition from human to wolf.

It was over.

Melinda laughed weakly. She had done it. She had willingly transformed herself into a werewolf outside of the moon's influence. However, she didn't felt the same rush of exhilaration as before. Instead, she was exhausted.

Shaking her body to throw off the leaves and dirt that had clung to her fur, Melinda lifted herself off the ground and stood on four legs. She raised her triangular head into the air and sniffed. The pungent scent of coal, the foul, mechanical stench of carbon monoxide, the subtle, earthy aroma of concrete, and the harsh, oily stink of tar filled her nostrils - there was a road to the east. Melinda sped off.

* * *

Melinda's mother rolled her eyes as she listened to her husband's rant. She briefly took her eye off the road to glance down at the vehicle's LED clock. It read 10:10 AM.

"I mean, it was bad enough he dragged us up to that shitty condominium in Denver instead of having the conference in town, but to take us on a tour of the place…gah, I don't want to think about it." Melinda's father shook his head in disgust. "He was so…damn, what's the word?…condescending. So he has a summerhouse? Big deal. "He puckered up his lip and took on a satirical, nasal voice. "'This is my fully equipped gym and swimming pool. Sent me back 10k, but you can't put a price on health.'" He spat out the open car window. "Asshole. Considering how fat he is I bet he never even uses the equipment."

Melinda's mother sighed as she turned the car along the street.

"I hope Melinda enjoyed her little vacation," she said.

"I'm sure she did," responded Melinda's father bitterly. "She didn't have to deal with that uptight fatass."

"You realize that uptight fatass is your boss, right dear?" said Melinda's mother absently.

"That doesn't mean I have to like him," he muttered.

"I suppose not," admitted Melinda's mother. "Just try to use a little more tact next time. Ah, here we are, home sweet home."

The Cooper van bounced gently up the curve and rolled smoothly onto the driveway and into the garage. Melinda's parents stepped out of the car and stretched.

"By the way, thanks for driving us back," said Melinda's father as he shut the car door.

"No problem," said Melinda's mother with a smile as she entered the house.

The door from the garage led directly into the laundry room. Melinda's mother walked in and put her purse down on the washing machine. She glanced around. Everything seemed to be in order.

"Melinda, honey! We're back!"

No response was forthcoming. Melinda's father entered the house, gently brushing past Melinda's mother. He dropped his heavy black briefcase on the sink counter with a grunt.

"I think she's still in bed," said Melinda's mother.

"Well I, for one, am starving," said Melinda's father, rubbing his hands. "Let's break open the fridge, the pantry, and get some breakfast. I could really go for some pancakes, OJ, maybe a little coffee."

Melinda's parents walked down the hall and into the kitchen, and froze. Their daughter was down on all fours draped in nothing more than in a dirty nightgown, furiously scrubbing the kitchen floor with a paper towel. A blue plastic bucket full of soapy water and a bottle of detergent were at her side. She was so focused on her task that she hadn't noticed their arrival.

"Ah, Melinda," said Melinda's mother with a sort of a fuddled bemusement.

Melinda yelped wildly and spun around. She stared up at her parents, and gulped.

"We're back," said Melinda's father, frowning. "Uhhh, wha-, what's all this then?" he said, waving his arms in the general direction of the glistening, wet kitchen floor.

"Um…um…" Melinda stuttered, opening and shutting her mouth. Her brain eventually caught up. "Power outage. There was this, um, power outage. Some of the food spoiled so I had to clean it up."

There was a long, awkward pause.

"Off the floor?" exclaimed her mother incredulously.

"What?" said Melinda.

"If the refrigerator was out of commission why would there be food on the floor?" persisted her mother suspiciously. "It's not as though it would fall out."

"Oh, no-no-no-no, it, uh, it…fell, last night - I-mean-this-morning - when I found out it went bad. I was going to throw it in the trash when I dropped it and it fell. I mean, some…liquids actually leaked out, yeah, that's it." Melinda shrugged helplessly.

There was another, longer, even more awkward pause.

"Hmm…is that so?" said Melinda's mother, folding her arms.

She stepped forward gave her daughter a long, hard stare.

Melinda shrunk under her withering gaze. What could she tell them? She didn't want to tell them the truth. She didn't know why she wanted to keep this to herself, but she did. She wanted to escape from this situation - to magically banish her parent's suspicion – but there seemed no way out.

"Shit," exclaimed Melinda's father suddenly.

"Eh?" said Melinda's mother, turning to him.

"It figures," he muttered, rubbing his temples. "All I want is a decent breakfast and boom, the fridge goes on the fritz." He sighed. "Ah screw it. Let's just go to IHOP or something; I was in the mood to eat out anyway."

"Dear?" said Melinda's mother. "Don't you find this a little…suspicious?"

"Suspicious?" said Melinda's father, bemused. "What do you mean? The fridge broke down. It's over twenty years old. Damn thing sounded like a rock grinder when the compressor was running."

Melinda's mother stared at him in disbelief.

"Melinda," continued her father, "Go up and get showered and dressed while we unload the van. I'll help you clean up when we get back from the restaurant."

With that said he stomped up the staircase, leaving Melinda alone with her mother.

Melinda stared up at her mother. At first, her mother seemed angry, but then, slowly, her scowl melted away. She walked past Melinda and opened the refrigerator door. She examined its contents.

"There's a lot of food missing," she said slowly. "All the soda, lunchmeat, and, oh, that big steak is gone. That was for dinner tonight, you know."

She wandered over to the pantry and looked inside.

"Hmm…all the beef jerky is gone. And the chips," she said. "Your father is the only one who likes those things." She looked over at Melinda and, to her daughter's surprise, smiled.

"What did you do last night?" she asked in an almost mischievous tone.

Before Melinda could respond her mother's grin turned to a concerned frown. She turned stiffly and walked to the liquor cabinet, opened it, and looked inside. A few seconds later she sighed with relief and shut the door.

"Good," said Melinda's mother. "If anything had been missing…well, we'd be having a different conversation right now."

"What?" said Melinda, thoroughly confused.

"Just finish cleaning up," said her mother, nodding at the floor. "Next time, if you want to have some friends over, just ask."

Not sure what to say, Melinda nodded dumbly.

"Come on, you slow-pokes," called Melinda's father from upstairs. "I'm starving."

* * *

The very first thing Melinda did after returning from the restaurant was check her calendar. Using a bright red marker she circled every full moon. She sat on her bed and cross-referenced the dates with her day-planner, flipping through page-by-page, month-by-month. To her relief none of them overlapped with any school activities, holidays, or other scheduled events - none-too-surprising considering how few she had planned. That task completed, Melinda paused to think.

If I'm going to keep this a secret, I'm going to have to be really careful. There's a full moon every thirty days or so… hmm…I wonder if it is the moon itself that triggers the change, or the moonlight? If it's the moonlight I might be in trouble.

She thought back to her experiences.

I really didn't change until I saw the full moon in the bathroom window…so I suppose the moon has to be in full phase to force the change. Maybe I can prevent my transformation by not exposing myself to the moon. Otherwise…I can more or less change whenever I feel like it!

Excitement ran down her spine. She could turn herself into a beautiful, powerful wolf-girl whenever she wanted.

Melinda took out a sheet of yellow notebook paper. She glanced at her bedroom door and began writing. She found that putting her thoughts down into words helped her think clearer.

1 - I can change whenever I want to, but it takes a lot of effort and energy…

Melinda paused, nibbling on the end of the eraser.

…when I have the chance I should practice transforming into and back from a werewolf.

2 - I will never voluntarily change when my parents are home and not asleep…

3 - Whenever I change I end up craving mass quantities of meat. I can't necessarily kill a deer every time I wolf-out - Melinda chuckled at the phrase - *so I'll have to find some alternative source of food.*

4 - I can't let anyone see me in my werewolf form. I especially can't let anyone see me change. The risk is simply too great.

5 - I need to determine what parts of the werewolf legend are true, and which are false. Can silver hurt me? Is merely touching it dangerous? I should make another list and perform the experiments when my parents aren't home.

6 - Are there others out there like me? Are there more werewolves in this town, this state, or even this country? I might be able to smell them in wolf form.

She leaned back and read what she had written thus so far. She felt like she was missing something important. Then, it hit her.

7 - Can I change other people into werewolves?

Melinda thought about this.

…Until I know for certain I should be very careful not to scratch, bite, or share blood with anyone.

There was a knock on her bedroom door.

"Honey?" said a muffled voice.

Melinda threw her calendar and notes under the blanket of her bed.

"Come in."

Melinda's mother entered. She leaned on the wall, giving her daughter a curious look.

"Uh, yeah mom?" said Melinda.

"Melinda," began her mother in a slightly concerned tone, "I just wanted to know if there's anything you feel you should tell me about yesterday night. You're a big girl now, and that means there are some things you can - and should - handle on your own. Your father and I don't have to be involved in every aspect of your life anymore. But there are still some things you will need help with. I think you're mature enough to tell the two apart."

Melinda reflected upon this.

"Thanks for asking, mom, but really, everything's fine," said Melinda.

Melinda's mother nodded gravely.

"That's all I wanted to say," she said. "I will not bring this up again unless you choose to."

She turned and exited the room.

Melinda sighed and fell down onto her bed. She glanced out the window into the sunlight. It looked like the start of a bright new day.

Chapter 4

The massive school bus slowly decelerated with a long, earsplitting metallic screech. The words "PINEBROOK SCHOOL DISTRICT" printed in bold, glossy black font on a bright yellow background scrolled across Melinda's vision. There was a loud hiss, followed by the dull mechanical whir of the bus door folding back, the engine still steadily running, spitting out billowing clouds of exhaust into the chilly morning air. The crowd of high school students standing on the sidewalk dutifully climbed into the rumbling vehicle.

Melinda sat down and placed her backpack on the vacant seat beside her, watching her schoolmates shuffle through the bus in a manner somewhat reminiscent of cattle being herded through a stockyard. They were all lugging large, heavy-looking backpacks; a few had those suitcase/backpack hybrids that could be rolled or carried. Most of them were half-asleep or just waking up.

Having received its passengers, the bus roared to life and sped down the quiet suburban street.

Melinda fidgeted restlessly in her seat. This would be her first day at school since her transformation. She wasn't nervous, but neither was she totally at ease. She was still coming to terms with what had happened to her and high school was hardly the ideal place for introspection. In fact, she had considered feigning a cold the night before so she could have another day to adjust. Far more worrying was the prospect of transforming in the middle of school. Though she hadn't shapeshifted since the morning after the full moon she wasn't sure how much control she had over her newfound power.

Melinda frowned, puzzled. Although she had ridden on the bus countless times there was something different today. Sounds were clearer and louder. Colors had a brighter hue. She found herself noticing little details around her that she would have normally overlooked or ignored - subdued yawns, quick glances, faint whispers, and more.

She glanced around nervously. She squeezed her fingertips and wiggled her toes in her shoes. Feeling no claws emerging from any of her digits she relaxed a little bit.

Melinda's nose twitched. She detected the faint scent of…rotting vegetables somewhere on the bus. She wrinkled her nose in disgust. The smell was already driving her nuts. She had to figure out where it was coming from.

Melinda rose from her seat. She slowly stepped through the aisle, garnering a few odd looks from the more attentive students. The smell led her to a backpack resting on a seat near the front. She bent to her knees and pressed her noise against the rough nylon fabric of the backpack, sniffing.

"Um…can I help you?" intoned a baritone voice.

Melinda jerked out of her trance. With a sinking heart she peered up. A tough-looking football player seated next to the backpack was staring down at her, a look of bafflement etched on his chiseled face. Melinda suddenly became aware that nearly everyone in the bus was now staring at her. Red hot, dizzying embarrassment washed over her. She managed a weak smile.

"The…the lettuce in your tuna sandwich has gone bad," she croaked.

The entire bus erupted into a chorus of sniggers and chuckles. Melinda meekly retreated back to her empty seat and remained there - eyes shut - for the remainder of the ride.

* * *

Yvette ran up to Melinda, who was standing in line in the school cafeteria.

"Hey Melinda!" she cried. "Is what everyone's saying about you true? Did you really sniff Greg McCloud's pants?" she asked with both awe and amusement.

Blushing, Melinda turned to face her.

"No, I didn't sniff his pants," responded Melinda staunchly.

Yvette chuckled.

"Are you sure?" she persisted.

"I think I'd remember that sort of thing," retorted Melinda in the same resolute tone.

"Then, how did the rumor get started?" asked Yvette, taking a food tray from the stack on the counter.

Melinda opened and shut her mouth, then sighed wearily, rubbing her temples.

"Look, all I did was…smell his backpack," she explained. "Don't ask me why. There was this really foul odor coming from it, see, and it was driving me nuts." She hesitated, noting the queer look Yvette was giving her. "It was early in the morning and I was sleepy, so I wasn't exactly thinking straight."

Yvette stared at Melinda, and smiled.

"Forget about it," she laughed. She patted her on the back. "Come on, it's no big deal. I bet it will be out of everyone's mind in a couple of days or so."

More like a couple of months, thought Melinda grimly as she reached for a food tray. What had come over her in that bus? It had been unbelievably humiliating and a little scary. Had she developed…instincts or something? Even while human?

"What's on the menu today?" said Yvette, scanning the food arrayed before them.

Melinda stared down at the steaming sunken metal trays. Corn, mashed potatoes, steamed broccoli, french fries, apples - nothing looked especially appetizing to her. Her gaze wandered over the pile of hamburgers wrapped in tin foil, and stopped. She hesitated, then reached down and placed four of them on her plate. She also took some of the steamed broccoli and a can of root beer - almost as an afterthought. After paying for her meal she took her usual seat at the back of the cafeteria with Yvette. She unwrapped all four hamburgers and then stared at them uncomfortably. After a while, she selected one of the burgers, removed its bun, and began chewing on the patty.

"Hey, uh, are you on a low-carb diet or something?" asked Yvette.

"Umm…yeah," said Melinda uncomfortably, reaching for a second patty.

"OK, but I don't think you need it Melinda," laughed Yvette. "You've been looking pretty good lately."

"Uh, thanks," said Melinda.

The two girls quietly ate their lunch together in the noisy bustle of the cafeteria. After a while, Melinda looked up uneasily at Yvette, who gave her a smile.

"Yvette," began Melinda hesitantly. "Have you, have you ever kept a secret from your parents?"

Yvette nodded. "Well," she began. "One time I went out with this skater. Everyone thought he was no-good, but he turned out to be all right, really. He just had a rough exterior. I didn't tell my parents I was seeing him at first, but later on I introduced him to them and they hit it off just fine."

"Oh, um, good then," said Melinda, not certain how to continue. "Why, um, why haven't I heard of him?"

"We broke up a while back," said Yvette. "Nothing nasty, just wasn't working out in the end."

"Oh," said Melinda, opening her can of root beer.

"Something on your mind?" inquired Yvette.

"Well, I…did you think it was the right thing to do - y'know, not telling them about him?"

Yvette cocked her head in thought. "Hmm…I suppose I should have told them," said Yvette. "The thing is I never actually lied to my parents. I just chose the right time to bring it up."

Melinda thought about this. Suddenly Yvette focused on something behind Melinda. Yvette smiled warmly.

"Oh, hi, girls!" she said.

Melinda groaned. Not again.

Cynthia, Heidi, and Lily rolled their eyes at Yvette' enthusiastic greeting while pretending not to notice it – a difficult feat. When they saw Melinda sitting next to Yvette, however, their mood changed instantly. Heidi and Lily broke into cruel smiles, while Cynthia scowled angrily. As one, the three girls sat up and approached the table Melinda and Yvette were sitting at. Melinda felt the hair on the back of her neck stand on end.

"Hi there," said Heidi, twirling with her gorgeous red hair.

Melinda gulped. She recognized that exaggeratedly saccharine tone of voice. They were up to something.

"How's it going?" asked Yvette, oblivious to the rising tension.

Ignoring her, Cynthia addressed Melinda, her hands pressed against her hips.

"I heard about what happened on the bus," she said menacingly.

Melinda gulped. Greg McCloud was Cynthia's boyfriend. How could she have forgotten?

"Um, look…" began Melinda.

"Who would've thought 'Linda here could be such a slut?" laughed Lily.

"Yeah, such a slut!" whispered Heidi none too quietly.

Melinda's face turned bright red. She noticed that the people sitting at the neighboring benches were watching the unfolding confrontation with no small interest.

Cynthia angrily turned to face her two cohorts.

"Shut up!" she spat. Heidi and Lily just chuckled.

"I only smelt his backpack, honest," murmured Melinda. "I wasn't-"

"Bullshit," growled Cynthia, folding her arms. "You know what really pisses me off? Greg said the whole thing actually turned him on a little. In case you didn't know, he's my boyfriend, and I don't appreciate little girls like yourself coming on to him."

"Hey, lookit what she's eating," said Lily, pointing at the hamburgers.

"Ooooh," cooed Heidi. "Trying to lose weight for Greg? Gotta look good for your new man, huh?"

"Hey, come on, she's telling the truth" pleaded Yvette.

"This doesn't concern you," said Lily sharply. "Do us a favor and stop talking for once."

"Look, I wasn't trying anything okay?" said Melinda defiantly, growing angry. "I'm not after him, Okay? Not interested."

"So, you're saying he's not good enough for you?" growled Cynthia. "You're just flirting with him?"

"Yes! I mean, no," stuttered Melinda. "I mean…"

Cynthia leaned over and whispered in Melinda ear.

"Nobody touches my Greg, especially not a skinny little bitch like you," she said furiously. "You'd better watch yourself, whore."

Melinda twitched. Her face turned bright red. People all around her were whispering and chuckling at her.

Then, something powerful and dark stirred inside her. Her hands curled into tight fists.

"Fuck…off," she whispered hoarsely.

"What?" breathed Cynthia incredulously.

Slowly, Melinda raised her head and stared defiantly into Cynthia's eyes. Years of tears, teasing and torment at her hands and others like her flashed through Melinda's mind. Tremendous rage boiled up from the depths of her soul.

"I said, *fuck off*," she growled, her voice suddenly guttural and bass.

Cynthia froze. When Melinda had spoken, her eyes had gleamed with a red light that inexplicably filled her heart with dread. Cynthia stepped back, trembling. Melinda's gaze swept over Heidi and Lily, whose expressions instantly turned from glee to terror.

"I…I…" stuttered Cynthia before regaining her composure. "W-Whatever," she gulped. "Just… stay away from him," she said weakly. "I'll…go now."

"You do that," said Melinda softly.

The three cheerleaders scurried away. Melinda gave one final growl and returned to her lunch. As she reached for her third patty, she noticed that the cafeteria had gone quiet. She glanced around and saw that everyone was staring at her. After a while, Melinda shrugged nonchalantly and took a bite out of her hamburger.

"Uh, Melinda, are you feeling all right?" asked Yvette, dumbfounded, as the sounds of conversation gradually filled the air once more.

"Never better," said Melinda, chewing contently.

A loud whistle echoed through the gymnasium.

"All right, line up! Time for roll call and warm-up!"

The crowd of uniformed students hastily queued up side-by-side. The high-pitched squeak of tennis shoes scraping against the floor filled the cavernous room. Coach McHugh - the P.E. instructor at Pinebrook High - watched impassively from behind his black sunglasses as the students fell into rank. Once everyone was in place, he raised his clipboard and began taking roll.

"Steven Gallagher?"

"Here."

"Marcy Penn?"

"Yeah."

"Fredrick Jorgensen?

"Yo."

Melinda was standing at the back of the line waiting to be called. She lolled her head back and stretched her arms, wondering what the hell had come over her during lunch. It wasn't as though it had been the first time Cynthia and her cronies had given her grief. The rage, adrenaline, or whatever it had been had worn off soon after she left the cafeteria, leaving her dizzy and disoriented. No doubt about it - something weird was happening to her. Her senses were slowly growing more and more acute. Mild cravings were becoming ravenous hungers. Her very being felt energized and alert to the point she couldn't stand still for longer than ten seconds. It was really starting to worry her.

"Melinda Cooper?" cried Coach McHugh suddenly.

Melinda blinked.

"Ah, here!" she said.

Coach McHugh put a little tick next her name on the roster. He surveyed the class one last time, and then spoke.

"Okay folks, you know the drill, five laps around the basketball court. Step outside the out-of-bounds lines and you'll be doing an extra lap."

The entire class immediately broke formation and started jogging around the court. Melinda sighed. Running - indeed, any physical exertion - was not her strong point. However, as she ran she found she was not at her usual position lagging at the back of the line. Instead, she was near the front. More to the point, she was enjoying herself. The sound of her heart pounding in her chest and the sensation of air flowing across her skin and hair was invigorating. She quickened her pace, moving up to the front of the line, and then far past it. Faint memories and images of her night in the woods flickered in her mind as she jogged.

"Hey, you can stop now; that's more than five," yelled Coach McHugh.

It took Melinda a few seconds to realize he was speaking to her. She slowed to a walk and took her place on the line next to the Coach, who was still flipping through the papers on his clipboard.

"You shouldn't wear yourself out like that, Ms. Cooper," he muttered, not bothering to look up. "You'll give yourself a heart attack."

"Actually, I feel fine, Mr. McHugh," said Melinda.

She felt great, actually. She hadn't broken a sweat. The run had been effortless. She felt as though she could've gone fifty laps or more.

"Well, you know your body better than anyone else," continued Coach McHugh skeptically. "Just be sure not to overexert yourself."

"I'll try not to, sir," said Melinda, holding back a smile.

Coach McHugh led them outside and onto the cracked, sun-parched black pavement of the outdoor basketball court. They assembled along the pull-up bars.

"Alright," the coach announced. "Today we're doing your second physical evaluation for the semester. You earn points based on how well you've improved since last time. We'll start with the pull-ups, then move on to curls, jump rope, and finish with push-ups. Then you can play basketball until the period is over. Get in line by alphabetical order, last name."

Everyone took his or her place. Being a Cooper, Melinda was among the first. When her turn came up she walked up to the bars and stared at them with trepidation. Last time she hadn't even managed one. She took hold, and flexed her arms with all her might. To her astonishment she shot up like a rocket, prompting a few gasps from the assembled students. She steadied herself and began rhythmically pumping her body up and down, up and down. Minutes passed. Finally, Coach McHugh called up to her.

"Okay, Okay, that's enough," he said, chuckling softly. "You're definitely getting an A+ for this part."

Blushing slightly, Melinda returned to the group. She couldn't help but notice that many of her classmates were staring at her in astonishment. She tried her best to ignore this.

Once everyone else had finished doing pull-ups Coach McHugh led the class back inside the gymnasium. Melinda sat down on the hard blue mat along with her fellow students and, at the start of the coach's whistle, fell back and started doing curls. She hadn't been too bad at them before, but now they were effortless. By the time the whistle sounded again she had lost count how many she had done but was certain she had more than doubled her previous score.

"Have you been working out at home or something?" inquired one of Melinda's classmates, who had been watching her in awe.

"Uh, yeah," said Melinda.

Next was jump rope. There were only ten jump ropes in the gymnasium so the class took the test in turns. When Melinda's turn came she stepped forward, gripped the handles and leapt into the air.

One.

Melinda yelped as the thick leather cord slapped against her insteps. Several nearby students chuckled. Cursing under her breath, Melinda stepped over the cord and tried again.

One. Two. Three. Four…

Now getting into rhythm, Melinda began to go faster.

Seven, eight, nine ten eleventwelvethirteenfourteenfifteen…

The students who had laughed at her were now staring dumbfounded as the jump rope blurred around her.

After everyone had finished they moved on to the final test – push-ups. Melinda lay down on her stomach, glancing around. More than a few students were watching her with interest. Deciding she ought to tone it down a bit, Melinda was careful to only do a little better than her previous best, putting on a show and trembling from false exertion as she performed her final push-up.

The bell rang about the same time the class finished, leaving no time for basketball. Melinda –tired, sweaty, yet strangely invigorated – jogged into the girl's locker room and sat down on the benches. She removed her shirt, exhaling heavily and shaking her head in weary amazement.

"Well…that was awesome," she said.

She had just worked out harder than she had in her entire life. It had been unreal. What was even more incredible was she had done all that with her willowy little body.

Hang on…

Melinda glanced down at her arms. There was something different about them. She flexed them. Though they hadn't gained any bulk almost every square inch of fat had been replaced by muscle, leaving them with a healthy toned appearance. The same went for her legs. Her stomach had always been flat, but now it seemed to have some definition. It was easy to see how she could have missed the change; in long pants and long-sleeve shirts she looked just the same as before. But take away the clothes and she looked positively radiant.

"I guess…I guess being a werewolf has its benefits," said Melinda.

Chapter 5

Melinda tapped her fingers on the kitchen counter, idly twirling her raven-black hair with her free hand. She glanced at the microwave's LED clock. It read 7:49 pm. With a sigh she leaned back - stretching her arms high into the air. Her neck and knuckles cracked softly as she extended her upper body, lifting her blue T-shirt to her midriff. She looked up at the staircase in the other room, her lips pressed into a frown of impatient anxiety. Finally, she raised her hand to her mouth and shouted.

"Mom! Dad! It's almost ten 'til eight! You're going to be late!" she called.

A muffled voice emerged from upstairs.

"We're more than aware of that, honey!"

Melinda groaned in frustration. She paced back and forth, occasionally glancing up the stairs, rolling her eyes. She absentmindedly opened the refrigerator and scanned its cluttered interior. Finding nothing of interest to her, Melinda shut the door and leaned back on the kitchen counter, resting her head against one the cabinets. After what seemed to be an eternity her ears perked up. Melinda scurried out of the kitchen and stood at attention besides the door leading to the garage.

Melinda's parents were dressed semi-formally, her father wearing a red collared long-sleeve shirt underneath a brown leather jacket with black dress pants and her mother draped in a white, knitted sweater, modest golden earnings, also wearing a pair of black dress pants. Melinda gave them what she hoped looked like an innocent smile.

"You have our cell-phone number," said her mother in a business-like manner. "We'll be gone until eleven, maybe even twelve. You're on your own as far as dinner is concerned; just don't order pizza."

"Oh come on," exclaimed her father in an exasperated yet disarming tone of voice. "Stop pretending you're trying to get her to cook for herself and admit you forgot to make something for dinner. Let her order a pizza if she wants; here, I'll give you a twenty," he began thumbing through his wallet.

"It's okay dad," said Melinda hastily. "I wasn't in the mood for a pizza. So, uh…you can go now."

"Oh, good girl," said her mother approvingly. "Just make sure you're careful. There's a fire extinguisher in the laundry room, and be sure to call 911 if-"

"Come on, dear, we're going to be late for the concert as it is," interrupted Melinda's father in a singsong voice.

"Yeah, you two should really get going," agreed Melinda, one step away from shoving them out of the house.

"Hmm, you really seem eager to get rid of us," laughed Melinda's father as he opened the door.

"She certainly does," commented her mother more seriously.

"Look, you guys have been looking forward to this thing all week, and uh, and I don't want you to miss it," wheedled Melinda, rather ineffectively.

Melinda's mother gave her daughter a look, and then a resigned sigh.

"Just be sure the house is still standing when we get back," said her mother, her voice now slightly more congenial.

"MOM!" protested Melinda. "You know me. What am I going to do? Throw a wild party?"

"No, the idea never came to my mind until now," said her mother dryly.

"Goodnight, mom," said Melinda, closing the door behind her.

Melinda sighed and pressed her ears against the door. She listened to her parents approach their car, open, and then shut the vehicle's doors. After a moment's silence the van's engine roared to life, as did the garage door opener. The sound of the car drifted away, soon followed by the rumbling grind of the garage door descending. Then there was silence.

Finally.

She jogged up the stairs and entered her bathroom. She flipped the light switch and opened the shades. The glaring, artificial radiance of the bathroom light blended with the subdued alabaster glow of the moon and stars. Melinda sat on the counter, checking her watch while she scooted up. It read 7:55 pm.

"I'd better give them ten minutes," she said to herself.

Fifteen minutes later she was still hesitant. She ran downstairs and checked the garage. It was empty. She searched every room in the house and shut all the windows and blinds. She even considered calling her mother on her cell phone, but decided against it on the grounds it might arouse suspicion. At last, she made her way back up the stairs and into the bathroom. She stared at herself in the mirror, and sighed.

"It's now or never," she said with equal measures of anxiety and excitement.

She locked the bathroom door just to be safe. She then turned her attention back to her image in the mirror. With a mild blush, she took off her T-shirt and jeans and placed them neatly on the bathroom counter next the sink. Next, she removed her shoes and pulled off her socks, rolling them into balls and sticking them in the back heels. Goosebumps formed along her skin as she stood there in nothing more than her panties and bra. The smooth, frigid bathroom tile floor chilled her bare feet. Finally, she slipped out of her undergarments and placed them along side her shirt and jeans.

It seemed odd to Melinda that she felt embarrassed about taking off her clothes in the privacy of her own bathroom. She had done just that no more than twelve hours ago for her morning shower. Perhaps the situation was making her uncomfortable; Melinda was very much used to taking off her clothes early in the morning, but not so she could transform into a werewolf.

Her physique had radically improved over the last two weeks. There was hardly an inch of fat left on her. Her skin had lost its sickly, pallid appearance - replaced by a healthy vibrant glow. Slender yet powerful muscles flexed all over her body whenever she moved. It was certainly a far cry from her former stick-like frame. The change had been so drastic that Melinda had been forced to take up weightlifting so that her sudden growth didn't appear entirely baseless. She had also toned down her performance in P.E. and started wearing baggy clothes to conceal her impressive new build. Her efforts seemed to have paid off; no one had noticed the startling change she had undergone - not even her parents.

There had been, however, one aspect of her evolving body she'd found difficult to hide: her eyes. For one thing, she didn't need glasses any more. One morning she had awoken to find she could see perfectly well without them.

Secondly, and more distressingly, her irises had turned from blue to green.

A week ago at school Yvette had asked Melinda if she was wearing green-colored contact lens. A quick trip to the girl's bathroom confirmed Yvette's observation; her eyes had adapted an unnatural aquamarine appearance. A panicked minute and a half later, Melinda was wearing a borrowed pair of sunglasses. Later she told her parents she had purchased nonprescription colored contact lens. They had been baffled by her decision but shrugged it off as yet another teenage fad.

She had no idea why it had happened but there was a lot she didn't understand about herself now.

This would be her first attempt to change into a werewolf since the last full moon. Even with her parents gone for the night, it was still risky. But if she wanted some measure of control over her new powers she needed practice. She took a deep, long breath, shut her eyes and stood perfectly still.

Her pupils dilated.

Melinda's skin rippled like water. Her limbs and torso began to pop and crack as though her bones were twisting around inside her. She groaned and fell to all fours. Her head drooped low, causing her dark black hair to cascade down her scalp, obscuring her face. Twitching uncontrollably, Melinda slowly raised her head - a low, menacing growl emanating from her throat. Her hair gradually parted, revealing a vicious, grinning, wolf-like countenance. Patches of ebony fur erupted all over her naked body. Claws burst from her swelling toes and fingers. A long, bushy black tail slowly pushed its way from between her legs and began to sway. Her limbs alternately shrunk and elongated, molding her form. Powerful balls of muscle ballooned within her arms and legs, filling and defining her figure. Gasping and growling, Melinda lifted her still changing body up, leaning on the bathroom counter for support.

It was like a stretch - painful at first, but over time the body got used to it. What had been agonizing was now merely uncomfortable, and what had been uncomfortable now felt almost good. The sensation of changing - of feeling herself swell with power, growing fangs, claws, a tail, thick fur, her senses becoming steadily more and more acute - was absolutely incredible.

At last, the transformation came to an end. Melinda howled long and loud, her ululation trailing off into the night. She rose to her feet, a werewolf once more.

Melinda immediately trotted out of the bathroom and padded down the staircase, making a beeline for the kitchen. She approached and opened the refrigerator door. Without hesitating she reached inside and grabbed an enormous, juicy steak. Licking her long chops, she bit into the meal with reckless abandon. Little droplets of red juice splattered across the kitchen floor in the wake of her feeding frenzy. The steak was gone in a matter of seconds.

Having satiated her hunger, Melinda now wanted to satisfy her curiosity.

She stepped into the dining room and approached a cherrywood cabinet set against the opposite wall. She reached down and tugged at cabinet's top drawer, opening it, revealing a glittering pile of silverware.

Melinda's own words echoed in her mind.

I need to determine what parts of the werewolf legend are true and which are false. Can silver hurt me? Is merely touching it dangerous?

Melinda gingerly reached over and touched one of her mother's prized silver-plated forks with her furry, talon-adorned fingers, then quickly retracted it.

Nothing.

Melinda eyed the fork cautiously as though it were trying to deceive her. Again, she reached out for the utensil, this time lifting it up between her lupine analog of a thumb and pointer. She examined the shiny treasure, carefully rotating it in her hand. She felt nothing.

Well, that was good to kn- Ahh!

Melinda dropped the fork to the floor with a whine, massaging her stinging palm. She looked down and saw an angry red welt where the fork had been. It hadn't hurt at first, but prolonged contact was downright unbearable – like touching red-hot iron.

Okay, thought Melinda in a daze. *I need to get rid of those silver earrings mom makes me wear for formal occasions.*

Grimacing, she picked the fork off the ground between two talons and flung it into the drawer as though it were a chunk of hot coal. She shut the cabinet violently, snarling at it for good measure. Stupid fork!

So…what next?

Melinda rubbed her furry chin. Werewolves were vulnerable to silver, but they were also said to be immune to everything else.

Melinda stepped back into the kitchen and rummaged through the drawers until she found what she was looking for: a short, serrated knife.

She held the blade over her left paw and, taking a deep breath, made a slit across her index finger. She yelped – more out of surprise than pain; the cut was deeper than she had intended. She looked down and saw a thin, glistening red line framed against the rough, hairy surface of her finger. Her nose twitched as she picked up the salty-tang odor of her own blood. After a few seconds what little pain she felt from the cut went away. Puzzled by this, Melinda walked over to the sink and washed the blood off her digit. When she had finished she carefully examined her finger and saw that the wound was completely gone; there wasn't even a scar.

"Wow," breathed Melinda. "I heal...really fast."

Melinda briefly considered putting her regenerative powers to a more strenuous test, but decided she didn't want to risk it. It'd be kind of hard to explain to her parents why she felt the need to lop off a finger. Besides, it still kind of stung.

"What else?" muttered Melinda to herself.

There really wasn't any way she could test whether she could pass her...condition to another person without actually attempting to do it, which was out of the question for the time being. The only other test she could think of trying was to see whether she had some special power over wolves. The only wolves around were in a zoo twenty miles away. She could put it off for another time.

Pausing to clean up the speckles of juice left from her dinner, turn off the lights, and lock the doors, Melinda disappeared into the night.

* * *

Melinda's quarry was tiring. It had put up a good fight but simply could not match her speed, agility, and endurance. She could have ended the chase ages ago but was having far too much fun. Panting, breathless, sweating, desperate to escape, it made a sharp left turn, hoping to throw her off and thus gain some precious distance. Unfortunately, Melinda saw the maneuver coming. She matched its sudden turn and added an extra burst of speed. She leapt into the air and with a snarl of triumph tackled it to the ground.

Grinning wickedly, she reached down and pulled her opponent's flag off his belt.

"Dammit Ms. Cooper, it's called 'tag' football for a reason!"

The excitement of the hunt evaporated. Melinda looked down and saw Steven Gallagher lying in the muddy grass, gasping for air. She hastily rolled off him and helped him up, apologizing profusely. The other team raised their voices in complaint while Melinda's teammates laughed and jeered at their opponent's plight. Coach McHugh blew his whistle.

"All right, that's the last down! Everyone get in position. You! Ms. Cooper! A word if you will."

Brushing the dirt off her shorts Melinda jogged up to Coach McHugh, who glared at her.

"Are you on the football team, Ms. Cooper?" he said slowly.

"Umm...no," responded Melinda, somewhat perplexed by the question.

"Are we practicing tackle football?" he continued.

"No...not really," said Melinda sheepishly.

"So, if we're not playing tackle football should you slam into your opponent or just pull the damn flag off their belt?"

"The belt. Look sir, it was just an accident, and it's not as if I hit him very hard-"

"Would you just sit down, Ms. Cooper?" interrupted Coach McHugh. "I have a game to run here, and I don't need tomboys like you treating their classmates like punching bags."

Melinda's ears reddened.

"I-It's actually okay, coach," said Steven, who hadn't minded having Melinda fall on top of him.

"Would you get back to your side, Mr. Gallagher?" snapped the Coach.

"Right, right," said Steven, backing away nervously.

Defeated, Melinda stepped gloomily towards the benches.

"Hey, wait a minute," cried a firm, female voice.

Melinda glanced behind her. A tall, freckled girl with dirty-brown hair was running towards the three of them. She pressed her hands to her hips and scowled.

"Why is she being benched?" she asked, pointing at Melinda.

"Look, you saw what she did, Christine," responded Coach McHugh wearily. "That has no place here."

"Yeah, well, I saw some of the guys tackling each other," she said angrily. "Why didn't you bench them?"

"Ahh, they were just messing around," said the coach dismissively.

"All right, they were messing around," said Christine. "Fredrick gives Carter a bloody nose and he's just messing around. She..." Christine waved in Melinda's direction "...just drags a guy to his knees and she's roughhousing?"

Coach McHugh sighed and rolled his eyes from behind his sunglasses.

"Christine, there's a-"

"She said she was sorry, he said he wasn't hurt, so what's the big deal?" interrupted Christine. "Is it because she's a girl?"

"Christine, we've had this talk time and time again..." replied the coach steadily, though now there was a hint of apprehension in his voice.

"Just tell me why you benched her when you let those jerks-offs get away with it?" she persisted.

Coach McHugh opened and shut his mouth. He rubbed the bridge of his nose and spat sideways into the grass. Finally, he nodded vaguely in Melinda's direction.

"Get out there," he leveled his pen at her, "But don't you start screwing around again. And I still want to see you after class, Ms. Cooper."

"Y-yes sir," gulped Melinda, who immediately turned and ran back out into the field. She took her position near the goal line, and was soon joined by Christine, who gave her a smile.

"You shouldn't let him push you around," said Christine, motioning towards the coach.

"He made a mistake and he knew it; he was just too embarrassed to correct himself."

"Pardon?" said Melinda, not quite understanding.

"He sees a bunch of the guys beating the hell out of each other, and hey, boys will be boys," Christine explained. "But the second a few girls start playing a little rough and...well, to him they stand out like a sore thumb. Coach McHugh's never gotten the idea of female athletes into that thick skull of his."

"Are you saying he's sexist?" said Melinda.

"Well, maybe a little," said Christine. "He doesn't hate women or anything like that. He just... expects guys to behave one way and girls to behave another way. When they don't...well, it kind of messes with his worldview."

"Oh, I see."

"By the way," said the girl friendlily. "I'm Christine".

"Um, Melinda," said Melinda, shaking Christine's hand.

"You're pretty good, Melinda," said Christine. "Do you play any other sports?"

"Me? Um, no, no, I don't actually play any sports."

"Could've fooled me," said Christine, more than a little astonished. "You were freakin' awesome."

"T-Thanks," said Melinda.

"Well, I'm on the women's lacrosse and soccer team," continued Christine. "You should consider trying out."

"I-I'd love to, but uh, I just don't think I'd have the time," responded Melinda, immediately realizing it was a lie. She had plenty of time. She didn't participate in…anything, inside or outside of school.

"Too bad."

Christine paused, as if considering something.

"You know, the big game against Asbury is tonight. A bunch of the girls from my lacrosse team are going to be there to root for the Wolves."

"The Wolves?"

"The Wolves. You know, our football team?"

"Oh yeah, them," said Melinda with a nervous laugh.

"I know you said you were busy, but can you drop by?"

"Well, I-I…" said Melinda hesitantly.

The shrill noise of Coach McHugh's whistle pierced the air.

"I-I-I'll be there!" yelled Melinda as the ball was hiked.

* * *

"What do you mean you can't take me?" cried Melinda desperately.

"I'm sorry, dear," said her mother as she powdered her face. "But your father and I have had this dinner date planned for almost a month."

"Couldn't you just drop me off at the school, then pick me up when you get back? I could wait." wheedled Melinda.

"We won't be getting back until one, Melinda," said her mother. "We're going to stop by a café afterwards for coffee with some old friends who are visiting town."

"I could hang around until one, please?" begged Melinda.

"For the last time, Melinda, no." Melinda's mother sighed and turned to face her daughter.

"Honey, I'm really sorry about this. If it were any other day I'd love to drive you there. I think it's wonderful you're making new friends and showing a little school spirit, but no."

Melinda's mother paused for a moment, as though considering something. Suddenly she snapped her fingers with a smile. "Hey, why don't you ask this new friend of yours to give you a ride?"

Melinda's mood brightened and then immediately darkened.

"I didn't get her phone number or email," she mumbled.

"Then I'm afraid you're out of luck, honey," said her mother, applying a thin coat of red lipstick. "I'm sorry."

Melinda cursed herself. She didn't know why she had accepted Christine's invitation - let alone why she was looking forward to it so much. It was just…no one like Christine had ever noticed her before. No one had ever invited her to their house, their birthday, a dance - not even to sit with them during lunch (well, except Yvette). She had convinced herself that she didn't like that sort of thing anyway. Well, now she wanted to try for herself.

She toyed with the idea of walking to the game. She knew the way to school and it wasn't as though Pinebrook was dangerous. But it was nearly an hour away on foot and she didn't want to walk home by herself at night.

Hang on.

Why should I *be afraid? I'm a werewolf, damn it! What could be scarier than me?*

Melinda stared into space.

She turned, walked down the hallway and entered her room. She sat at her desk logged on to her computer, opening a map of Pinebrook. Rolling the mouse wheel, she zoomed in until both the wildlife preserve and Pinebrook High were in view. She traced a route with her finger from the school through the preserve…

…To her house.

The wildlife preserve bordered the school soccer field. If one could cut through the preserve it was only two and a half miles away.

Making a decision, Melinda stood, walked back to her parent's room and tapped her mother on the shoulders.

"Hey, uh, I just got a message from Christine on Facebook," said Melinda. "I asked her if I could get a ride to the game and she said yes."

"Oh, wonderful," said Melinda's mother happily, putting on an earring. "When is she going to pick you up? I'd like to meet her."

"Uh, she didn't say," said Melinda quickly. "I'm waiting for her."

"Well, if I miss her be sure to say hi for me," said Melinda's mother absently.

"Sure," said Melinda, nodding.

As Melinda walked away, she realized she was getting good at lying to her parents.

* * *

Once her parents were gone Melinda dumped her textbooks out of her backpack and replaced them with supplies – a bottle of water, cell phone, two changes of clothes, a watch, flashlight, compass, paper and pen, map of the area, twenty dollars plus some change and a packet of beef jerky. She'd come up with it one night as she lay in bed thinking about the harrowing morning after her initial transformation and swore she'd never leave the house as a werewolf without it.

After scanning the perimeter of her high school on the computer she had determined that the safest, least conspicuous route to the campus involved cutting through the preserve from the north, following Mayberry road until she reached the soccer field. From there she could slip into the empty storage shed (they never locked the doors) change out of her fur and into her clothes and make her way to the football stadium. According to Yvette – who attended these things religiously, apparently – the school grounds were virtually abandoned during a big game night like this one, so no one would see her… hopefully.

This would be the most harebrained, irresponsible, and arguably dangerous thing she had ever done. There were so many ways it could go wrong. Someone could spot her going to or leaving the game. She could lose control and shapeshift in front of the entire school. Her parents could figure out she never got a ride from Christine. Why was she doing it? Was it her werewolf side? Though the physical aspects of her transformation were obvious she couldn't dismiss the possibility that her personality had changed as well. The mere fact she was actually going through with this crazy scheme was proof enough - not to mention that little encounter with Cynthia, Heidi, and Lily in the cafeteria.

Melinda shook her head and continued packing.

"This will work," she reassured herself. "It's…really no different from walking to the game. I'm just taking a shortcut." She hesitated. "And…changing into a seven-foot-tall furry freak there and back," she finished lamely.

She was silent.

"I can do this," she snarled. "I'm not going to be scared of anything anymore. Not my parents, not school, not Cynthia."

She zipped her backpack shut and threw it on her bed. She turned, locked her bedroom door, lowered the blinds of her windows, and started to undress. She tossed her shirt, undershirt, pants, bra, socks, and panties in the laundry hamper. Now fully nude, she stood up straight and nodded.

"It's werewolf time," she whispered to herself.

There was a trick, Melinda had learned, to triggering the change outside of the moon's influence. It wasn't enough to want to be a werewolf. For one brief moment she had to believe she already was one. She had to surrender herself entirely, recalling every sensation and emotion of the experience – the thick coat of fur, the wet nose, sharp talons beneath her fingers, a tail wagging behind her rump. Then, something would happen to her that she could barely describe. It was like…growing a second set of muscles; she would feel an incredible potential blossom within herself. All she had to do then was release the potential – flex the muscles – and the transformation would begin. And once it had begun there was no stopping it.

Melinda shuddered as a familiar warmth filled her. She fell to the floor but quickly scrambled back up on all fours. She inhaled and exhaled long and slow, trying to relax her body. Stress and fear made the process all the more painful so the best thing to do was stay calm and let the transformation run its course.

The bones in her face and neck cracked and popped as her nose and jaw slowly pushed outwards, forming the initial growth of her muzzle. Wicked, dark claws burst forth from her soft, pink toes and fingertips. She stretched her long, toned legs, watching them bulge and twitch with a mixture of fascination and disgust. Her skin suddenly itched intensely as patches of dark fur erupted all over her. Within a few seconds the burgeoning growth of fur covered her entire body. Her muscles – now quite respectable – began to swell. Her biceps grew to the size of cantaloupes. Her flat stomach rumbled ominously, and then quickly hardened. Her calves and ankles ballooned outward as her legs and feet slowly shifted into a digitigrade stance. She growled wildly as her tail slowly pushed its way out her backside. Her nose darkened. Her nostrils flared back. Her gums bled as long, sharp predatory fangs replaced her dull canines. Her piercing green eyes swirled to yellow and began to glow with an inner light. Her short crew cut grew into a long, wild mane.

She howled.

Melinda stood up and shook her head, stretching her enormous, furry body. She yawned, displaying an impressive array of glistening, razor-sharp teeth at the fore of a cavernous red mouth with a great long tongue. It irked her that she always howled at the culmination of her change, but she couldn't stop herself from doing it. Sooner or later the neighbors were going to start complaining.

Melinda gingerly picked up her backpack with a clawed paw, readjusting the straps so that they would fit over her massive shoulder. She chuckled; she certainly made for an odd sight – an enormous she-wolf carrying a tiny pink backpack.

She trotted down the stairs and crept into the kitchen, keeping her head low. A bright white light suffused the room as she opened the refrigerator. She helped herself to a steak she'd picked up at the supermarket; last week her mother had commented that the meat in the house was rapidly disappearing so Melinda had started purchasing her own supply. Once she had finished her meal she slid the screen door open, stepped outside, and shut it behind her. Falling to all fours she slipped out the back gate and began weaving her way through her neighbors' backyards, heading towards the preserve. It was actually the safest portion of her trip to the school. As long as she stuck to the hedges and bushes she was basically undetectable. The tricky part was the entrance to the wildlife preserve at the cul-de-sac. There was no cover around the gate and the adjoining sidewalk was brightly lit by a nearby streetlight. The only option was a mad dash to the forest from one of the yards.

Melinda took a deep breath and darted across the street. She shot through the gate and sprinted into the forest. No one saw her.

The wildlife preserve had nearly been demolished by a developer several years ago. After a protest from a local environment group nearly shut down the state capital the county had opted not to sell, leaving the land untouched. At the time Melinda hadn't paid much attention to the drama, but now she was thankful the preserve had been saved. Putting aside how beautiful it was at night, she couldn't imagine what she would have done on her first full moon as a werewolf if it hadn't been there.

Several miles onward Melinda lifted her long canine nose into the crisp evening air. She picked up the strong, greasy stench of fried food, sugary drinks, and many excited people. A cursory glance at her surroundings confirmed that she was moving parallel to Mayberry road. She was en route. Minutes later, Melinda's triangular ears perked up. She slowed to a brisk trot, stealthily clinging to the shadows of the trees. The forest gradually became less and less dense until at last it gave way to the empty school soccer field as well as the welcoming sight of the storage shed. It was about fifteen to twenty yards out in the open. Melinda darted artfully from tree to tree until she was at the very edge of the woods, and then made a dash across the field to the shed. She hurried inside, carefully but quickly shutting the flimsy wooden door behind her.

The interior of the shed was dusty and choked with cobwebs. Several half-inflated, mud-caked soccer balls lay scattered on the dirt floor. Rising to her feet, Melinda stretched her wide muscular shoulders and neck, grimacing when she realized she was still hungry. She dug into her backpack and retrieved the packet of beef jerky. She ripped the plastic covering off and devoured its contents. All the seasonings and sauces made the meat taste odd to Melinda's lupine palate but it was better than nothing. She tossed the empty packet to the ground and, after a quick glance outside, stood up straight and shut her eyes, concentrating.

Changing back to her human form could be either very easy or very hard. She never had any trouble transforming back into her old self at the end of a long night out in the woods. Conversely, it was nearly impossible for her to revert to human from just after adopting her werewolf shape. She was neither tired nor noticeably energized, so she wasn't sure how difficult changing back would be. After a few tense seconds, Melinda felt her fur begin to recede. Her muscles deflated, her claws softened into fingernails, her tail disappeared into her body, and she shrunk back into her human form. Shivering in the chilly night air, she quickly pulled her shirt, pants, panties, bra, and sweatshirt out of her backpack and began dressing. Using the shed's solitary window as a mirror she adjusted and combed back her hair. Satisfied with her appearance, Melinda zipped up her backpack and headed towards the football stadium.

* * *

The stadium was absolutely packed. There was hardly a single open seat in the stands and the field was teeming with fans and athletes. Melinda couldn't believe that a high school football game could attract so many people. How was she supposed to find Christine and her friends in this throng? She could barely even remember what she looked like.

"Hey, MELINDA!" called someone.

Melinda blinked.

"Over here!"

It was difficult to make out the voice over the roar of the audience. Melinda anxiously scanned the crowd ahead of her until she caught sight of a hand waving in her direction. Attached to the arm was a familiar, smiling, freckled-covered face.

"There you are!" said Melinda, running over to her.

"Did you have any trouble getting here?" asked Christine.

"Uh, nope," replied Melinda.

"Great! Let me introduce you to the team."

"The team?"

Christine led Melinda through the bustling crowd. She guided her through the shifting press of bodies until they were near the field. Rows of towering stadium lights positioned behind the stands kept the play area as bright as day. Cheerleaders danced and chanted on the sidelines in their bright, shimmering outfits while the players ran about in their mud-speckled uniforms, frantically chasing after the football, tackling each other, and generally raising a ruckus.

"Uh, wow, this is…this is…a lot," said Melinda, overwhelmed.

"First time out to a game?" asked Christine as they slipped past an overweight couple standing by the bathrooms.

"Yeah," said Melinda, trying not to breathe as they passed the toilets.

"Well, if the Wolves beat the Cougars tonight we'll be going on to state, so practically everyone at the school is here," Christine explained distractedly, standing on her toes, searching for something in the sea of heads.

"I…didn't even know the Wolves were on track for state," said Melinda, bewildered.

"You're kidding, right?" laughed Christine. "There was a pep rally just last week."

"I, er, never go to those things," said Melinda. "I just hide out in the library until it's over."

"Really? Ah well, no big deal," said Christine distractedly, still peering into the crowd.

Suddenly, Christine smiled broadly and waved her hands.

"Ah, hey girls! I'm back," called Christine.

Melinda looked in the direction she was waving and made out a group of six athletic-looking girls sitting at the bottom the stand in front of her. Half of them were wearing red and white uniforms. They greeted Christine warmly.

"This," said Christine, motioning to Melinda, "Is Melinda. I met her in P.E. and she said she wanted to check out the team."

"Hello," said Melinda, waving diffidently.

She was met with a chorus of greetings.

"Here, why don't you sit next to Tiff here?" said Christine to Melinda. "Thanks for saving the space, by the way."

"No problem-o," said Tiffany.

Melinda sat down on the chilly aluminum bench and turned her attention to the game. Her knowledge the sport was limited to her experience playing touch football during P.E. so she was a little out of her element. She recognized her school's team - the Wolves - by their distinctive red and white uniforms and the howling wolf silhouette painted on the side of their helmets. They were playing against the Sunsdale Cougars and winning by a small margin. Suddenly, the ball exploded from the scrimmage line. It cut a high arc, spinning lazily in the air until it was caught by one of the Wolves, who was then immediately tackled by several brutish-looking Cougars. The referees' frantic whistling filled the air as the crowd groaned.

"It was the last down," explained Christine, sensing Melinda's confusion.

"Oh, right," said Melinda. "That means the ball goes to the other team."

Melinda watched the players slowly walk along the field to take their positions.

"So, Christine said you were interested in playing lacrosse?" said one of Christine's teammates, addressing Melinda.

"Me? Oh, well, I never actually gave it much thought," said Melinda.

"Considering the way you moved in flag football…well, you'd be a natural," said Christine.

"Thanks," said Melinda, blushing.

"Hey, I've seen you in P.E. before," said another one of Christine's friends. "Up until a month ago you were kind of on the wimpy side."

"Hey, Melody, what the fuck?" laughed Christine, playfully punching her on the shoulder.

"What?" chuckled Melody. "She was wimpy. Now she's, like, an Olympian or something." She turned to Melinda. "How'd you get in shape so quick huh? What's your secret?"

"Oh, er, I just started working out every day – at least one hour, no exceptions," said Melinda quickly. "And uh, my parents got me a personal trainer. I just…I wanted to get in shape."

"Well whatever you did, it worked," said Melody.

"Yeah," said Tiffany. "Christine was right; you'd make a great addition to the team."

Melinda glanced at Christine, who looked guilty.

"Hey, hey, don't get me wrong," said Christine. "I didn't invite you to the game just so I could pressure you into joining…okay, maybe a little," she admitted. "But if you're not interested we can still hang out."

Melinda considered this. She didn't know much about lacrosse, but this was the first time any clique had shown interest in her. Christine and her teammates seemed friendly enough. Plus, being on a sports team looked good on a college application.

"Well…when's practice?" she asked.

"We start at 3:30 - right after school - and play until around 5:00," replied another member of Christine's team. "A bunch of us usually stick around for another half-hour or so for a few quick points, but that's only if we have enough players and enough time."

"We aren't playing any other teams for a couple of months," continued Christine. "That'll give you plenty of time to learn how to play. Hey, you want a hamburger or something?"

"Oh! Yes, please," said Melinda eagerly. "Make it two…and uh, and a diet coke or something."

"I'll get 'em," said Tiffany, who disappeared into the crowd.

Melinda and the rest of the girls turned back to the game. It was exciting to watch, even if Melinda wasn't all that into football. It also presented her with an opportunity to test her enhanced sense of smell. One thing she had discovered over the last few weeks was everyone had their own unique scent. Some people had very similar scents – particularly if they were blood relatives – but no two were exactly the same. It was hard to isolate any one scent in such a large crowd, particularly with so many other odors wafting in the air. She shut her eyes and inhaled deeply. She mentally sorted through all the aromas, trying to identify them. The first one she recognized was Christine's, followed by Greg McCloud's. She looked up and spotted him on the field. Satisfied, she took another sniff, and then frowned. The scent was familiar, but she couldn't quite place it.

"Hey Cynthia!"

Melinda froze.

"Hey Christine," said Cynthia distractedly as she walked past, followed by Heidi and Lily. All three were wearing their cheerleader outfits. They looked stunning.

"Have you met Melinda?" called one of Christine's friends.

Cynthia stopped mid-step; Heidi and Lily nearly collided with her. She slowly turned around and stared at Melinda, who stared back.

"What is she doing here?" said Cynthia, making little effort to hide the disdain in her voice.

Melinda narrowed her eyes. A growl escaped her lips.

"Uh, we invited her," said Christine, bemused. "Do you, uh, already know each other?"

"We've met," said Melinda gravely, rising.

"Yeah," said Cynthia.

Christine frowned.

"Wait a minute," she said. "Wasn't there some kind of…fight between the two of you in the cafeteria?"

Christine folded her arms.

"Yeah, 'Linda here was getting fresh with Greg on the bus," she said, glaring at Melinda.

"For the hundredth time, it was a misunderstanding," said Melinda angrily. "He's a great guy but he's yours and I'm not interested."

Cynthia lips tightened. For a moment she locked gaze with Melinda but quickly looked away, twitching. Melinda grinned triumphantly. She still wasn't exactly sure what she had done to Cynthia at lunch, but clearly Cynthia hadn't forgotten.

"Fine, whatever," said Cynthia.

Lily and Heidi stared at her in mild shock.

"Cynthia! You sa-" protested Lily.

"What abou-" said Heidi.

"Drop it," hissed Cynthia, silencing them. She nodded at Melinda.

"So, you joining the lacrosse team now?" she asked in a carefully neutral tone.

Melinda looked over at Christine and her team, who had been watching the confrontation with interest.

"Yeah," said Melinda as casually as she could manage.

"That's cool," said Cynthia. "Maybe we'll see you out on the field some days."

Melinda blinked. There was no sarcasm or edge to Cynthia's voice.

"Uh, thanks, yeah," said Melinda, amazed.

Suddenly, Melinda's ears perked up. Someone in the crowd was calling her name.

"Melinda! Hey, hey, Melinda!"

Melinda turned around and scanned the crowd. A small figure was carefully but quickly sliding between the press of bodies towards her. It was Yvette.

"Oh God, here we go," sighed Cynthia, who had also spotted Yvette's approach.

"Who is it?" asked Christine.

"The bane of my existence," said Cynthia.

Yvette emerged from the crowd and ran over to the group, almost tripping over herself in her haste.

"I thought I saw you in the crowd," said Yvette, laughing. "But I then I said to myself 'she never comes to these things' so I stopped looking but then I was looking for you, Cynthia, and saw Melinda sitting here so I was like 'wow, I can't believe they're all here.' So great to see you all down here!"

"Um, hi Yvette," said Melinda anxiously.

"Hi Melinda, hi Cynthia, hi Heidi, Lily!" said Yvette with almost maniacal excitement.

"Hi crazy bitch," muttered Heidi not quite under her breath.

"Sorry, who are you?" said Yvette, addressing Christine.

"This is Christine, Yvette," said Melinda. "We met at P.E. She's on the lacrosse team."

"Hi Christine!" said Yvette brightly, extending her hand.

"Uh, hey there Yvette," said Christine slowly.

"I've seen you girls on the field playing lacrosse," exclaimed Yvette. "It's a great game! I'm surprised more people aren't into it." She turned to Melinda. "So, are you here with the girls to support the team? Thinking about joining the cheerleading team? I told you that you should try out, Melinda! Maybe I co-"

"Yvette!" barked Melinda, raising her hands. "Calm down."

"Ah, sorry, sorry!" said Yvette, grinning foolishly. "Just…so great to see you all down here."

"Yeah, you mentioned that," said Lily dryly.

"I've invited Melinda to come with me over and over again, you know. I'm glad she's finally come. So, who do you think is going to win, huh? The game's pretty close, but the Cougars are-"

Grimacing, Cynthia stepped forward, nodding at Melinda.

"Uh, Melinda, could I talk to you for a second?" she said in an exaggeratedly cheerful tone.

Before Melinda could reply Cynthia took her by the arm and dragged her over to a gap between two bleachers, leaving Yvette and the lacrosse team behind.

"Look," sighed Cynthia as the two teenagers stood in the shadows. "Could you convince your… friend to go somewhere else?"

"What?" said Melinda.

"She's being more irritating than usual," said Cynthia. "It's giving me a migraine. Get rid of her, OK?"

Melinda stared at Cynthia.

"Look," began Melinda. "I know Yvette can be a little…enthusiastic but-"

"Enthusiastic is a goddamn understatement," snorted Cynthia. "She annoys the fuck out of me," she glanced over at the lacrosse team. "And Christine by the looks of it."

Melinda peered through the rows of seats, spectators, and support beams and spotted Yvette and Christine. Yvette was talking and laughing, Christine was smiling wanly; a few of her teammates were rolling their eyes or whispering to each other.

"She's just being friendly," said Melinda, feeling a spark of anger.

"Being friendly, huh?" said Cynthia, smiling nastily.

"Jesus, it's not like that."

"That would explain why the two of you were always hanging out."

"Watch it," snarled Melinda, stepping forward.

Cynthia backed away.

"Hey, easy," she said, raising her hands. "Settle down there, butch."

Melinda growled. She swore she could feel claws forming beneath her fingertips.

"I'm not asking you to tell her to fuck off," said Cynthia wearily. "Just…get her away from us. I guess you can stay. Christine seems to like you – God knows why."

"I wasn't aware I needed your permission," hissed Melinda.

"Oh, cute," said Cynthia, grinning. "You grew a backbone." She suddenly scowled. "Look, I don't know what the hell is going on with you, but don't think for a second I wouldn't sabotage things with you and the lacrosse team."

"What?" exclaimed Melinda, nonplussed.

"Christine has been asking around about you," continued Cynthia. "I haven't said anything yet, but when she hears about what a slut you are, how you've been whoring around with half the football team…"

"Don't you dare," breathed Melinda. "If you do I'll…"

"You'll what?" said Cynthia, folding her arms.

Sputtering with rage, Melinda was about to respond when she shivered. Her hands were aching and she was starting to feel unbearably hot. Sweat was trickling down her brow. It was almost like she was…

"Oh no," whispered Melinda to herself.

"What? Huh? What are you going to do?" snarled Cynthia.

Fighting back the urge to rip Cynthia to shreds, Melinda stumbled back and leaned against one of the support beams. Motes of light were flashing in her eyes; she could feel her hands and fingertips swelling up.

Need to calm down, Melinda thought desperately. *Got to relax. Deep breaths.*

"Hey, what the fuck is wrong with you?" exclaimed Cynthia with a strange mixture of concern and contempt.

Melinda breathed in and out, clutching the cool metal beam tightly with one hand. Seconds passed like eons. Gradually, the heat dispersed. Her inflamed hands shrank down to their normal size.

Melinda sighed, relieved. She glanced over at Cynthia, narrowing her eyes. She stood up, grinding her teeth. Then, she sagged, sighing once more.

"Fine, I'll get rid of her," muttered Melinda.

"Huh?" said Cynthia, bemused.

"I said I'll get rid of Yvette," said Melinda glumly, staring down at the ground. "Just…lay off, OK? I'm *really* not in the mood for this shit tonight."

"Oh, well, good," said Cynthia, quickly regaining her composure. "Hop to it."

"Yeah, whatever," muttered Melinda, walking past her.

Melinda stepped out from under the bleachers. She turned and gazed at Yvette, who was still chatting with the team. Shaking her head dejectedly, she approached Yvette.

"Hey, Yvette?" said Melinda, smiling weakly.

"Oh, hey Melinda!" said Yvette brightly. "I was just telling the girls about your little, ah, adventure in the park. I hope you don't mind."

Melinda winced inwardly as unwanted memories flashed in her mind but shook her head.

"No, it's fine," she said.

"Hey, where did Cynthia go?" asked Yvette, peering around Melinda. "I wanted to ask her something."

"Um, er, Yvette…can I talk to you for a second? Alone?" said Melinda.

Yvette blinked.

"I…suppose so," she said, puzzled.

"Good," said Melinda. She turned and addressed Christine.

"This will only take a second," said Melinda, almost apologetically.

"Uh, sure," said Christine slowly. "Nice to have met you, Yvette."

Melinda led Yvette along the bleachers until they were a good distance from the lacrosse team.

"Yvette," began Melinda uncertainly. "The thing is…"

"Is…everything alright, Melinda?" asked Yvette curiously.

Melinda bit her lower lip. Try as she might she couldn't come up with a convincing excuse or lie.

"Thing is…" said Melinda. "This…Christine invited me to watch the game with her and the team."

"So…?" said Yvette, confused.

Melinda squirmed.

"It's…getting kind of crowded over there," she managed.

"What?"

"Can you just…watch the game somewhere else?" pleaded Melinda. "I'm…I'm asking you as a friend…" she trailed off as she realized how horrible it sounded.

Yvette stared at Melinda

"Is…is this because I told them about what happened to you in the park?" said Yvette after a while. "I mean, I know you asked me to not to talk about it, but it's been nearly two months and-"

"No! No, it's not that," interrupted Melinda, raising her hands.

"Then, why do you want me to go?" asked Yvette quietly.

Melinda was silent. Around them, the spectators stood up in their seats as the Wolves scored a touchdown. The roar of the crowd echoed throughout the stadium.

"It's OK, Melinda, I understand," said Yvette suddenly.

"Wh-what?" said Melinda.

"You made some new friends and want to spend some time with them," said Yvette quietly. "I'll head to the other side of the stadium."

Yvette had an expression on her face that Melinda had never seen before – sorrow, tinged with bitterness. Melinda felt a knot form in her throat.

"Look, Yvette…" began Melinda hoarsely.

Without saying another word Yvette turned and stiffly marched away, disappearing into the crowd. Melinda stood there. Then, she felt someone tap her on the shoulders and whirled around as though she had been caught doing something shameful.

"Whoa, everything all right?" said Christine, cocking her head.

"Um, yeah, I guess," said Melinda weakly, rubbing the back of her neck.

"Where did your friend go?"

"Um, she's…she's going to watch from the other side," said Melinda miserably.

"Whatever," said Christine, shrugging. "C'mon, Cynthia and some of the other cheerleaders are taking a break and are going to watch the game with us. Oh, Tiffany finally came back with your food. Sorry for the wait, but there was a huge-ass line," laughed Christine.

"Yeah. Thanks," said Melinda, glancing back at the crowd as the two of them walked back to the bleachers.

* * *

Pinebrook lost in the end. Though the Wolves had the edge in terms of strategy and teamwork the Cougars were bigger, faster, and meaner. Their defeat didn't sour the evening for Melinda nearly as much as her less-than-cordial parting with Yvette.

Despite this, Melinda enjoyed the game. She particularly enjoyed hanging out with Christine and her friends. Melinda had always assumed that athletes were an uncomplicated lot with few ambitions and interests outside of sports. As it turned out she had a lot in common with them. They read the same books, took many of the same classes and listened to the same music. They were also some of the nicest, friendliest people Melinda had ever met. Cynthia and her cronies kept their distance for the rest of the evening, though every so often Melinda spied Lily or Heidi staring sullenly in her direction.

After the game Melinda chatted with Christine and her team in the parking lot as they waited to be picked up. Christine's parents were the last to arrive. She waved goodbye to Melinda through the open window of her father's truck as they drove out onto the street.

"See you at practice!" she yelled.

"I'll be there!" replied Melinda earnestly.

Melinda stood there for a while, watching Christine's car disappear into the night. Most of the spectators had already left. The stadium lights were rapidly fading. She checked her wristwatch. It read 11:48 PM.

"Better get going," she murmured to herself.

She walked across the parking lot crossed the chain-link fence and stepped out onto the soccer field, humming contentedly to herself. Aside from the unpleasant business with Yvette her gamble had paid off. She'd made new friends, established a truce of sorts with Cynthia, and, more importantly, had a blast. With any luck she could make amends with Yvette tomorrow. She thanked her lucky stars that there had been food at the stadium; otherwise she wouldn't have the energy to transform again.

She arrived at the storage shed. She reached for the knob and turned it only to find the door had been locked.

"Shit," hissed Melinda.

Melinda glanced around uneasily. She looked back at the high school and then the stadium. There were still some spectators and students hanging around so she couldn't risk changing shape on campus. Besides, the janitors took extra precautions during game nights, locking every entrance to the building to discourage vandalism; there wouldn't be any place to hide.

She glanced back at the shed and the not-so-distant forest.

"Screw it," she muttered to herself.

She slipped behind the side of the shed facing the woods. Giving her surroundings one last careful look she undressed and stuffed her clothes into her backpack. Shivering in the cool night, she shut her eyes and focused. A few seconds later she felt the metamorphosis begin.

"Melinda?"

It was Yvette.

Melinda's bowels turn to ice. She spotted the glow of a flashlight coming from the other side of the shed. She sniffed the air and picked up Yvette's scent, confirming what she already knew.

"Are you there, Melinda? I saw you walking out here," said Yvette.

Melinda pressed her changing body against the shed, cursing under her breath. How the hell had she snuck up on her like that?

"Hello? Hello?"

The light grew brighter.

"Rrrrrr….go away," barked Melinda, wincing when she heard how deep her voice had already become. "I…I'm peeing, okay?"

The light stopped moving. There was silence. Then, Yvette spoke.

"Why are you going to the ba-…" Yvette trailed off, sounding frustrated. "You know what? Never mind."

Melinda shuddered in pain. She glanced down at her hands and saw they had already grown claws.

"Listen, Melinda, I…couldn't leave the school without saying something," began Yvette.

Melinda moaned softly. Her limbs cracked and stretched as fur grew all over her nude form. Her head arched back as she felt her face stretch out into a short muzzle.

"You…you really hurt my feelings," continued Yvette from the other side of the shed. "I think it's great you're friends with Cynthia now, but… the way you brushed me off…I thought we were friends too."

Blood dribbling down her lips, Melinda fell to the ground. She pounded the dirt, screaming. No matter how hard she resisted she couldn't stop the transformation – merely delay it. And the longer she delayed it the more agonizing it became.

"Wh-what was that?" yelped Yvette.

Melinda covered her mouth. Her wild yellow eyes darted back and forth searching for an escape route, but it was too late. The transformation had reached its climax. She could barely think straight now, let alone run away.

Melinda howled in anguish as her body expanded. Muscles bulged along her arms, legs, chest, and back as her burgeoning coat of fur grew thicker and fuller. Her ears flared outwards and then narrowed into pointed tufts as they traveled up her skull. Her muzzle lengthened. Sharp teeth erupted from her darkening gums. Her eyes flared with an inner light as her pupils dilated and her irises shifted from green to golden yellow. Below, a lump formed on the small of her back as her coccyx swelled beneath her skin, eventually pushing out and forming a tail. When her change was finally complete Melinda rose from the ground, shaking her head in confusion.

"M-Melinda?"

A bright yellow light shone directly in her face. Melinda raised a furry paw to shield her eyes, growling in annoyance.

"Oh *Mon Dieu*…"

Melinda froze. With a sinking heart she slowly lowered her paw and looked down. Yvette was standing a couple yards away, staring at her in horror.

"Y-Yvette," said Melinda hoarsely.

Yvette immediately stepped back, clutching her tiny flashlight.

"S-s-stay away!" she cried.

"It's okay! It's me!" pleaded Melinda in her deep voice.

Yvette continued to back away. Her eyes were wide and her skin had turned white.

"No! No! Just hold on!" continued Melinda desperately, stepping towards her.

Yvette gasped. She turned around, looking at the forest and back at Melinda, trembling.

"Just WAIT!" growled Melinda.

With a terrified scream Yvette dropped the flashlight and ran.

"YVETTE! COME BACK!" roared Melinda with equal parts anger and panic.

Yvette did not respond. She reached the edge of the soccer field and disappeared into the trees. Melinda snarled, fell to all fours and scampered into the woods after her.

The forest was darker now. The distant lights of the town were fading and the pale glow of the gibbous moon overhead barely penetrated the cover of leaves and branches. Up ahead, Melinda made out a small figure stumbling through the gloom. It was Yvette – her scent was unmistakable.

As Melinda ran, something curious happened. The dread that had gripped her since Yvette discovered her hiding behind the shed slowly ebbed. Despite everything that had happened she was starting to feel surprisingly good. The sounds and smells of the forest and the sight of the moon in the sky were stirring something inside her – something wild and wonderful. Though initially apprehensive of these feelings, Melinda quickly surrendered to them. After everything she had been through at the football game she just wanted to let loose. She accelerated, tongue lolling out of her mouth, reveling in the thrill of the hunt.

Before long she was mere inches away from Yvette. She bunched her body up into a tight ball and sprang into the air, tackling Yvette and dragging her to the ground.

Yvette thrashed about, weeping and screaming.

"*CALM DOWN*!" bellowed Melinda.

Melinda pinned Yvette to the forest floor and stared into her tear-filled, quivering eyes with her own glowing yellow orbs. She felt no resistance. A not-so insignificant part of her relished the feeling of power – to dominate another so utterly.

"Listen," hissed Melinda. "I-"

Yvette reared back and bit her on the left paw.

Yelping in pain, Melinda withdrew her paw. Yvette tried to squirm away but even one of Melinda's paws was more than enough to hold her down.

Melinda did not know what drove her to do what she did next – rage, frustration, panic, or instinct. Roaring, she opened her massive, tooth-filled maw and seized Yvette' neck.

The scream echoed throughout the forest and beyond.

Melinda felt blood trickle through her mouth. When her tongue registered its bitter tang her eyes widened. Suddenly disgusted, she spat out Yvette' neck and pushed her away. The terrified girl shot to her feet and ran screaming into the woods.

Melinda just sat there, staring into space, dumbfounded.

"Why?" she whispered into the cold, unfeeling night.

Chapter 6

The bedroom door swung open. Melinda staggered inside, naked save for the tattered pink backpack she carried, which she promptly tossed on the floor. She reached into her closet and pulled out a thick white bathrobe. After wrapping it around her body she hurried over to her bedside cabinet and started scrabbling around the top drawer, searching for something. A few seconds later she retrieved a cell phone charger and shut the drawer.

"Why…didn't I check…the power…before leaving?" gasped Melinda as she unwound the cord and plugged the charger into an outlet.

She reached over for her purse and took out her cell phone. She grabbed the end of the charger and stuck it into the phone's USB port. An ersatz tune filled the room as the phone booted.

"Come on, come on," muttered Melinda to herself.

After what seemed an eternity a menu appeared on the screen. Melinda accessed her contact list, selected Yvette's cell phone number, and pressed 'send.' She raised the phone to her ear.

The ring tone buzzed once. Then twice. Then three times. Finally, Melinda heard Yvette's automated voice mail prompt.

"Shit," growled Melinda, hitting the 'end' end button.

Melinda brought up Yvette's contact entry again but this time selected her home phone. The ring tone buzzed once, then twice, but this time she heard a click as someone picked up the phone.

"Uh…yes," intoned a tired female voice.

"Y-Yvette?" said Melinda hopefully.

"N-No, this is her mother, Antoinette," said the voice with a French accent.

"Oh, yes, Mrs. Montague," said Melinda nervously. She'd only met the woman a couple of times.

"Wait, is this Melinda?" said Mrs. Montague.

"Yes," said Melinda.

"Why are you calling about my daughter? Do you…do you know where she is?" asked Mrs. Montague hopefully.

Melinda opened her mouth, and then shut it.

"Hello? Hello?"

"I…I last saw her at the game tonight," said Melinda slowly. "I…wanted to make sure she got home safe."

"She's not here, Melinda," sighed Mrs. Montague. "Oh my, I'm really getting worr-…"

Then, Melinda made out the sound of a door being opened over the phone, followed by a cry of joy.

"Mrs. Montague? Hello?" cried Melinda.

All she heard was muffled static followed by a loud thud. Then, two frantic voices talking in what she could only assume was French.

"Hello? HELLO?" repeated Melinda in confusion and fear.

A couple seconds later Mrs. Montague spoke.

"Oh, so sorry, Melinda, but Yvette just came home!" she said happily. "I dropped my phone when I saw her."

Melinda's heart leapt.

"Can I…can I speak to her?" she asked anxiously.

Melinda heard Yvette say something over the phone.

"Oh, it's just Melinda, Yvette," said Mrs. Montague, apparently addressing her daughter.

There was silence.

"What's wrong Yvette?' said Mrs. Montague. "Yvette?"

Melinda heard a succession of thumping sounds.

"Yvette? Why are you running? Yvett…oh, OH! Is that blood on the floor? YVETTE!"

Melinda stood there in frozen silence.

"Forgive me Melinda but I…I have to go," said Mrs. Montague desperately. "Yvette is hurt. Goodnight."

There was a click. Melinda slowly lowered her phone and dropped it.

"Shit," whispered Melinda quietly.

How had everything gone to hell so quickly?

She sat down on the bed and started thinking.

Yvette was obviously scared out of her mind, and rightfully so. She might be willing to talk once she had a chance to calm down, but what if she said something to her mother in the meantime? What if she called the police? The FBI? Granted, they probably wouldn't believe that a werewolf attacked her, but the bite on her shoulder was real. All Yvette had to do was point her finger and her secret life could unravel before her eyes.

Melinda shivered as she recalled the moment she sank her fangs into Yvette's flesh. It had been like her confrontation with Cynthia in the cafeteria, only this time she had done something far worse than bruising a bratty cheerleader's ego. Though Melinda was by nature reserved she wasn't emotionless. She had experienced anger, joy, jealousy, sorrow, frustration, and so on – all the emotions a teenage girl might feel at one time or another – but never so *intensely* as she did now. It had to be her transformation; it was definitely affecting her mind. She wasn't sure she could go on living like this – where trivial things could enrage her beyond reason.

Maybe it would get worse. Maybe it was only a matter of time before she was reduced to nothing more than a wild animal.

She glanced down at the phone on the floor, and shook her head sadly. She put the phone on the cabinet, turned off the lights and crawled into bed. It was quite a while before she drifted off to sleep.

* * *

Melinda shut her locker's door. She pinched the bridge of her nose and rubbed her face, sighing. Her skin felt greasy despite the fact she had showered no more than four hours ago and her head felt like it was stuffed with cotton. She glanced around at the crowd of high schoolers making their way down the main hall to the cafeteria.

Having nothing better to do she pulled out her cell phone, dialed Yvette's number again and again an automated voice told her the party she was calling was not available. Melinda pocketed her cell, cursing under her breath. Either Yvette's phone had run out of power or she had shut it off. She couldn't summon the nerve to call Yvette's home phone for fear that she had told her mother what had happened to her out in the forest.

Melinda wrinkled her nose in disgust as a pair of girls passed by. The combination of perfumes and hairspray the two were wearing was making her want to retch. Ahead she picked up a whispered conversation between three skaters regarding a cruel prank they played on a freshman during the football game. Melinda turned away only to catch a whiff of marijuana. Gagging, she peered through the crowd and spied a stocky male teen furtively passing a tiny plastic bag to a tall, prim, redheaded girl. The voices, smells, and motions around her seemed to grow in intensity. Every detail, every laugh, whisper, footstep, grunt, odor, and gesture blurred into an excruciating sensory barrage. Feeling faint, Melinda shut her eyes, held her breath, and covered her ears.

THUMP

Something heavy collided with her, knocking her against the lockers. Blinking in surprise, Melinda opened her eyes and saw a pudgy male student with a scraggly goatee walking away, oblivious or indifferent to the fact he had nearly bowled her over. An angry snarl escaped Melinda's lips. She steadied herself and started marching towards her assailant.

Melinda stopped mid-step.

"No," she hissed to herself. "Keep it together, keep it together…"

Gradually, the red mist left her vision. She sighed wearily, shaking her head. Maybe she should just call in sick. Give Yvette (and herself) a day to cool down.

Then, she picked up another scent, and for some reason it instantly drew her attention. It was strange – sour, musky, but not unpleasantly so, with an "aftertaste" Melinda swore she'd encountered before. Curious, she sniffed the air. The smell was getting stronger. In fact, it kind of reminded her of…

"Yvette," Melinda whispered.

She turned. The crowd of students was already thinning. A small figure was half-walking half-limping down the hall. Melinda strode forward, pushing her way through the mob, and then gasped.

It was indeed Yvette, but the girl hardly looked like herself. Her normally cheerful face was pale and sullen, almost grim, her gaze downcast, a hint of fear in her eyes. Her hair was a tangled mess, her undershirt was sticking out and her bra straps were hanging loosely from her shoulders. She walked with a strange, limping gait as though half her body had become as stiff as wood. But the oddest thing about her, at least to Melinda, was her smell. People emitted a spectrum of odors that could change slightly depending upon their mood, but Yvette's was radically different from what she remembered.

"Yvette!" cried Melinda, waving her hand.

Yvette stopped. She slowly looked up at Melinda. Her lips curled into something approaching a fearful scowl. Melinda narrowed her eyes. At first it looked like Yvette was wearing a turtleneck but she realized with a sinking heart that her neck was covered in bandages.

Melinda hurried over to her.

"I've been trying to get a hold of you all day," she said anxiously.

For a moment Yvette looked as though she was going to run away, but then she sighed and shrugged diffidently.

"Well, you have me…again," she said softly.

"We need to talk about…what happened last night," said Melinda awkwardly.

"I…I'd rather…we didn't," said Yvette, fidgeting.

"What? No! Please!" pleaded Melinda. "I'm trying to help y-"

Without warning Yvette shoved Melinda against a locker. The metal door rattled violently in its frame as her body made impact.

"Help me? *Help me?*" sneered Yvette. "You…you…"

Yvette trailed off. She lowered her gaze to the floor, grimacing as though suddenly very ill. She took a step back, clutching her forehead. Melinda stood there, stunned. In all the years she'd known Yvette the girl had never done anything remotely violent.

Yvette slowly looked up at Melinda. Trembling, Yvette raised her hands. They were swollen and red. Tiny veins and arteries were throbbing beneath the inflamed skin. Melinda stared at them in horror.

"What did you do to me?" whispered Yvette in a terrified voice.

Melinda furrowed her brow. Something was very wrong here.

Then, she remembered.

…Can I change other people into werewolves?

"Y-Yvette," managed Melinda, mouth agape. "Could you…could you lift the bandages off your neck? Just for a second?"

There was silence. Then, Yvette reached up and peeled back the upper portion of the wrappings, exposing the skin underneath. Although there were some brownish-red stains in the bandages themselves there was no injury – not even a scar.

"It was like this when I woke up," said Yvette quietly. "I showed my mother and…and I told her I was fine. I…didn't want to go to the doctor. How did you…how did you know?"

Melinda slapped herself on the forehead. Yvette's rapid recovery, her fever, her mood swings, her scent – it all added up. Why hadn't she figured this out sooner? How could she have been so stupid?

"Listen, Yvette," said Melinda. "Just…calm down, OK?"

Yvette's nostrils flared.

"Calm down?" she hissed. "I've been…*mon Dieu*, I've been *trying* to stay calm all morning, but… but…"

Tears rolled down Yvette's flushed cheeks. Sniffling, she wiped them with her sleeves.

"Yvette," croaked Melinda, reaching for her.

Yvette slapped Melinda's hand.

"STAY AWAY FROM ME!" she screamed.

The hallway suddenly went silent. Melinda looked around. Everyone was staring at them. Face red with embarrassment, she turned back to Yvette, who looked even more discomfited by the sudden attention.

"Yvette, I…I wasn't going to hurt you or anything," said Melinda, trying to ignore the whispering. "Why did you…?" Melinda trailed off, gesturing weakly at her.

Yvette's expression fluctuated between resentment and shame.

"I...I don't...I don't know," she managed. "For Christ's sake, Melinda, I called my mother a...a stupid bitch this morning when she told me I shouldn't go to school. Please, make it stop!"

Melinda stared at Yvette. Nothing like this had happened to her after she had been bitten. True, she had been a bit feverish the night before her first transformation, but-

She gasped. The full moon was tonight!

There had been a two week gap between the time she had been bitten and the full moon; Yvette had been bitten less than twenty-four hours ago. Maybe the transition from human to werewolf was more traumatic if it took place over a shorter period. Maybe stress exacerbated the process. Maybe the change was simply more painful for some people. Whatever the reason, Yvette clearly wasn't adjusting well.

This could be bad.

"Listen, Yvette," began Melinda anxiously. "We...we need to get you out of here."

"What? W-Why?" said Yvette. "You...you still haven't told me what's happening."

Melinda bit her lower lip.

"Well, you see..." she began.

"Hey, Melinda!"

Melinda shuddered. She turned around.

Cynthia, Heidi, and Lily had emerged from the crowd of onlookers. Cynthia glanced at Melinda, and then Yvette, a wicked gleam in her eye. Heidi and Lily snickered.

How do they keep sneaking up on us like that? thought Melinda grimly.

"Hello, Cynthia," said Melinda.

"Something wrong here?" asked Heidi in an innocent-sounding voice.

"We're fine," said Melinda between grit teeth. "Just...talking about the game last night, all right?"

"Oh, sorry," said Cynthia, stepping forward, twirling her blonde hair. "It's just...we heard screaming and wanted to see what the fuss was all about."

Melinda knew where Cynthia was going with the conversation and didn't like it in the least. She glanced back at Yvette and to her dismay saw that the girl actually seemed relieved by the appearance of the three cheerleaders.

"It's nothing, okay?" said Melinda dismissively, stepping between Yvette and Cynthia. "Just a...a disagreement. Between the two of us. Nothing to worry about."

Cynthia nodded.

"Oh, I understand," she said. "Probably for the best, though."

"W-What are you two talking about?" said Yvette, confused.

Cynthia smiled cruelly for a moment and then cupped her mouth in mock surprise.

"Oh, I thought you already explained the situation to her," she said. "Last night at the game, I mean. Why you don't want to hang out with her anymore."

Yvette gasped. She stepped around Melinda and faced her.

"Wait, is...did she...did you...is she?" stuttered Yvette, pointing at Melinda and then Cynthia.

Melinda's lips tightened. She turned her head to the side, avoiding Yvette's gaze, ashamed.

"Melinda...how...how could you?" breathed Yvette.

Cynthia patted Melinda on the back.

"Look, it's nothing personal, Yvetta," she said smugly. "But, hey, no hard feelings, right?"

"Get away from me!" hissed Melinda, pushing Cynthia away. "It's not like that!"

"Hey! The fuck?" said Cynthia as she was forced back.

"You told me to get lost!" growled Yvette, marching towards Melinda. "You told me you didn't want to hang out anymore!"

"No! I never said that!" protested Melinda, raising her hands. "I only asked you to…to…"

"Melinda wasn't the only one who was getting sick of your blabbering, Yvetta," said Lily. "I mean, the whole lacrosse team an-"

"Lily!" barked Cynthia.

"Ah, sorry," meeped Lily.

"W-What?" exclaimed Yvette in shock. "You girls were in on this too?"

Yvette stared at Cynthia with a pleading look in her eyes. Cynthia frowned, clearly annoyed, and then gave a dramatic sigh.

"Oh, fuck it," she said, folding her arms. "It's not like we're hiding the fact you annoy the hell out of us, Yvetta. We asked Melinda here to get rid of you and she did. Deal with it."

Yvette's mouth slowly widened as Cynthia finished. There was a long, terrible silence, broken only by whispers and chuckles from the crowd of gawking students. Then, lips trembling, tears welling in the corners of her dark, sunken eyes, Yvette spoke.

"It's not Yvetta; it's Yvette," she said softly.

"Yvetta, Yvette, Yve, who the fuck cares?" snorted Cynthia.

Melinda watched the unfolding scene with a mixture of rage, humiliation, and helplessness. She stepped towards Yvette, hand raised, opened her mouth, but no words emerged. She slowly lowered her hand in silence.

Smirking triumphantly, Cynthia nodded at Heidi and Lily.

"Come on girls, looks like Melinda and Yvetta here have som-"

With a sound somewhere between a snarl and a scream Yvette hurled herself at Cynthia. Cynthia yelped in surprise and tried to push her away.

"LET GO YOU LITTLE FREAK!" shrieked Cynthia.

Melinda rushed forward, grabbed Yvette by her waist and tried to pull her away but Yvette's hold on Cynthia proved surprisingly strong. Heidi and Lily followed suit, each one seizing one of Yvette's arms, but even their combined effort couldn't break Yvette's iron grip.

Suddenly, Yvette growled savagely and bit Cynthia on the arm.

Cynthia howled in pain. She pounded Yvette's head repeatedly but Yvette just bit down harder. Eventually, Cynthia crumpled the floor, whimpering in agony, giving Melinda, Heidi, and Lily enough leverage to yank Yvette away from her. Cynthia huddled against the lockers clutching her wounded side, face screwed up in pain. Blood was running down her skin.

"Jeez, she's got some kind of crazy retard strength!" gasped Lily, struggling.

Then, Yvette turned and – blood dripping down her lips – bit Lily on her upper arm. The cheerleader screamed and relinquished her hold. Moving with frightening speed Yvette twisted around and bit Heidi as well, who held on for a few seconds before letting go with a cry of pain.

Snarling, Melinda leaned back and squeezed Yvette as hard as she could. Melinda swore she heard something crack. Seemingly unaffected, Yvette stomped on Melinda's right foot. Melinda screamed in agony as Yvette broke free and ran, knocking several astonished onlookers aside.

Melinda staggered down the hall towards her.

"Yvette! Come back!" she cried.

Yvette disappeared around a corner. Cursing, Melinda limped after her. Behind, students were crowding around the injured cheerleaders, some helping, most just gawking.

Melinda eventually made it to the end of the hall and turned where Yvette had run. To her horror she saw the school parking lot through a side exit, its door wide open. Several teens were standing nearby, looking perplexed.

"Did you see a girl run through here?" barked Melinda.

"Uh, yeah," said one of the students, bemused. "She, uh, ran out of the door. We saw her heading towards the soccer field."

Melinda had already dashed out the doorway. Following the scent of blood she circled around the main building and found herself standing on the edge of the field that bordered the forest. Several PE classes were in session. Groups of teens wearing white T-shirts and grey sweatpants were jogging or running along the periphery while others were on the grass doing sit-ups or pushups under the supervision of the coaches. Melinda looked around but saw no sign of Yvette. She desperately sniffed the air but the presence of so many active, perspiring bodies made it impossible to tell which direction Yvette had gone.

She stood there for a couple of minutes and then slowly turned and walked back to the school in a sort of terrified trance.

As she re-entered the main building she heard a commotion down the hall where she had confronted Yvette. She hurried – still slightly limping – towards the sound and was greeted with the sight of a small mob of students and faculty. Melinda pushed her way through the crowd and saw the school nurse attending to Heidi, Lily, and Cynthia's injuries. A small first aid kit lay open on the blood-speckled floor.

"Ow-…OW OW! Easy, lady!" hissed Cynthia.

"Sorry, I'll take it slower," said the nurse as she applied the bandage, wrapping it around the cheerleader's wounded arm.

"Yeah, well-"

Cynthia suddenly looked up at Melinda.

"There you are!" she said angrily. "Where the fuck did she go? Huh?"

All eyes turned towards her. Still dazed, Melinda opened her mouth to speak but froze. She wrinkled her nose.

"Excuse me," said one of the teachers. "Is what they're saying true? Did a girl named Yvetta…bite them?"

Melinda paid no attention. She breathed in deeply through her nostrils, focusing on the extremely faint yet unmistakable odor now wafting in the air – sour, musky, but not unpleasantly so.

It was the scent of a werewolf. But this time it wasn't Yvette.

Melinda stared at Cynthia, her gaze running along her right arm and then fixating on the blood-stained wrappings.

Chapter 7

Cynthia wiggled her shapely legs as she drew up her white pantyhose. She looked up and there - leaning against the wall next to the showers in the otherwise empty gym locker room – was Melinda, a look of grave concern on her face.

"You?" groaned Cynthia. Lily and Heidi looked up from their lockers and rolled their eyes.

"Yeah, me," said Melinda quietly.

"Look," began Cynthia after a while. "Not in the mood to talk right now. Go away."

Melinda frowned, gazing downwards.

"Sorry, but, we need to talk," said Melinda.

Cynthia rolled her eyes.

"Fuck off," said Lily. "Bad enough your girlfriend went psycho on us."

Melinda's face turned beet red.

"She went 'psycho' on you because yo-..."

Melinda stopped herself mid-tirade, took a deep breath, and continued.

"Just for a second, okay?" she said in strained voice.

Cynthia turned to Lily and Heidi, who, after a moment's consideration, shrugged. She turned back to Melinda.

"Fine. Talk."

"Where to start," began Melinda uncertainly. "Uh, how are you, uh, how are you girls feeling?"

There was silence.

"You're kidding, right?" said Cynthia.

"No!" hissed Melinda. "It's important!"

"Well, now that you mention it my arm feels like some crazy bitch used it like a chew-toy," spat Cynthia angrily. "Has she had all her shots? I'd hate to catch crazy bitch."

"So, you also feel mad, stressed out, maybe a little nauseous?" persisted Melinda, trying not to smirk at Cynthia's last remark.

"Uh, yeah," said Heidi. "Who wouldn't be? The nurse said there's a chance we'll need stitches!"

"You won't."

Heidi glared at Melinda.

"Believe it or not, I really hope they track her down soon," remarked Cynthia. "Can you believe she ran out into the forest? Anyways, they'll probably pick her up in a day or two. Can't wait to see her get expelled...hell, I might talk daddy into suing her ass."

"She was under a lot of stress," said Melinda crossly. "You three treating her like shit didn't help."

"Like we treated her any different from how we always do," snorted Cynthia. "You're the one who's supposed to be her friend. 'Sides, it's no excuse for biting us."

Melinda winced. She stared down at the floor, lips pursed, and then nodded curtly.

"You're right," she said quietly.

She looked up.

"But the whole...biting thing, that's what I wanted to talk about," she said with sudden urgency.

Cynthia rolled her eyes and shook her head in disgust.

"You know what? Don't want to hear it. Don't care. Get out."

"I'm trying to help you!" exclaimed Melinda.

"You heard her," snapped Lily, pointing a thumb at the doorway. "Fuck off."

Melinda glanced uneasily up at the overhead windows. It was getting dark. She checked her watch.

"The thing is, Yvette-" she began.

"Oh SHUT UP!" growled Cynthia, stepping forward and pushing her just as she was looking up.

Melinda stumbled back and collided with the hard tile wall.

"Let's get one thing straight," snarled Cynthia. "I don't like you. I've never liked you and I never will like you. And I don't need a reason why. But for the sake of argument here are a few: You're an annoying, nerdy little bitch who put the moves on Greg, made us look bad in front of the entire school, and you're friends with Yvette Montague – the most insufferable human being on the planet. You get in good with Christine and the rest of the dykes on the lacrosse team and suddenly think you have a shot at being queen B. Don't make me laugh. You keep this shit up and I will destroy you just like I destroyed Yvette. Now, get the fuck out of my sight!"

There was a long silence.

Melinda quivered with rage. Blood was pounding in her ears. The beast was roaring at her. It wanted to shut them up for good. It wanted to tear them to ribbons. It wanted to pound them to a gory paste.

Then, memories of the night of the football game flashed in her mind – memories of Yvette's terrified face. The rage slowly drained away.

Melinda brushed her shoulders and addressed the three cheerleaders.

"Fine, I'll go," said Melinda softly. "Sorry for bothering you."

Cynthia and her cronies looked somewhat surprised but didn't question this unexpected victory.

"Fine, I'll go," mimicked Heidi in a nasal voice. "Sorry for bothering you."

"See you at school tomorrow, 'Linda" cooed Lily.

Melinda turned as if to leave, and then looked back at the three cheerleaders with a calm, resigned detachment.

"You girls are real bitches, you know that?" she said quietly.

Cynthia snorted.

"Yeah, well, it takes one to know one," she said.

Melinda paused. She smiled wanly.

"Yeah, I guess it does," she said.

* * *

As she watched the three cheerleaders change into their clothes Melinda wryly wondered whether she was the first female peeping tom in the school's girls' locker room.

She had ducked behind the laundry cart adjacent to the showers after her confrontation with Cynthia and the others. It was the perfect hiding spot from which to observe them. Granted, it smelled horrible, but Melinda was not going to miss this – not for the world.

The windows above the locker room were translucent and polarized, allowing only a limited quantity of moonlight inside. It was much like her first shift in her bedroom, where moonbeams filtered through the shades. She could easily restrain her body's inclination to change in such low background light. The three girls, however, lacked such control. Their transformation was going to be slow and painful, which suited Melinda just fine. They could deal with what was about to happen on their own. And seeing their reaction to their new shapes would be priceless.

Of course, once it was over she'd have to take matters into her own hands and lead them out into the nature preserve. It might get a little messy, but she felt strangely confident she could handle all three in their transformed state. They would be disoriented, confused, driven by instinct; she could work with that.

She wondered what they would look like. Would they resemble her or would they take a slightly different form? For that matter, when would the change start? It had been nearly a half-hour and-

"What the hell?"

Melinda's head shot up. Cynthia had taken a seat on one of the benches next to the lockers. She was fanning herself with both hands. Heidi was standing a yard to Cynthia's left behind a different row of lockers. She was rubbing her forehead.

It's happening! thought Melinda.

* * *

Cynthia took a deep breath, brushing her long, blonde hair. She shifted her knees uneasily, feeling the polyester fabric of her red skirt rub against her thighs. Her skin had developed a bright red blush that gave her the appearance of having just stepped out of a hot shower. Her ruby-red fingernails danced up and down on the worn wooden bench.

"God, I feel like shit," she murmured.

She ran her fingers through her flowing golden hair and then shook her head. She stood up, and, feeling dizzy, steadied herself on the closest locker. Her breathing was becoming more rapid and shallow by the second.

"Heidi," croaked Cynthia, her head drooping. "Could you…could you drive me home? I think I'm coming down with something."

There was no response.

Cynthia gritted her teeth, cursing under her breath. Her head was pounding and her cheerleader uniform was beginning to feel extremely tight - almost as though it were shrinking.

"Heidi?" repeated Cynthia, slowly raising her head.

"Cynthia," groaned Heidi. "I-I feel hotter than hell."

Cynthia glanced over at Heidi, who was also leaning against a locker, her chest heaving up and down as she breathed in and out. Her skin had turned almost as red as her hair. Her forehead glistened with perspiration.

"Jesus, you too?" moaned Cynthia.

"Yeah…maybe it was something we ate," muttered Heidi uneasily.

"Or…maybe that crazy bitch really was sick with something," added Cynthia nervously.

"AAHHHHHH!"

The scream had come from the showers.

"Lily!" cried the two girls in unison.

Cynthia started limping towards the showers but an intense pain erupted in her legs.

"GRRRHHHHHHHHH!"

She fell to her knees and curled up into the fetal position. Heidi rushed over to help her but groaned in pain and tumbled down beside to her. The two writhed in pain on the frigid tile floor, clutching their hands, which had become swollen and inflamed. Suddenly, their fingertips bulged. Fractures formed along their well-manicured nails until they splintered into pieces.

Long, dark, glistening talons erupted from their bloody stumps.

Cynthia stared at her hands and screamed in horror. She scrambled to her feet, nearly falling back to the floor as claws burst from her toes, ripping through her socks. Hearing a moan she stared down at Heidi's recumbent form. She was shaking and heaving, her tangled red hair splayed across the floor like a mop. Then, as though molded by unseen hands, Heidi's nose peeled back and slowly grew outwards, darkening as it expanded. As Cynthia watched the grotesque process she realized she was scratching herself. A powerful itch was creeping up her legs, chest, back, neck and arms. She reached up to scratch herself and heard the sound of fabric tearing. Cursing, she looked down and saw that her clawed hands had torn through her outfit like it was fishnet.

Heidi's body was growing larger and larger. A tear had formed at her collar and was slowly moving down her midsection, heralded by the sound of hundreds of minute polyester threads snapping. Soon Cynthia was experiencing the same wardrobe malfunction. She fumbled for the zipper of her uniform but couldn't reach it. Cynthia hesitated, and then with a roar of frustration tore her dress off with her newly formed claws. Shreds of red and white fabric flew everywhere.

Cynthia stared down in shock. Her entire body was covered by a thin layer of blonde hair. The hair began to thicken and curl. It darkened to brownish-yellow. Mere seconds later, she was covered in thick fur. Below, Heidi had grown a russet-colored pelt that gradually lightened to near crimson on her front.

Just as she was coming to grips with this alarming new development she felt a piercing sensation centered on the small of her back. Cynthia stared down at her rear. A tiny bulge had appeared on her coccyx. It grew outwards, stretching the white material of her undergarments. Finally, it popped out of the top.

It was a long, bushy yellow tail.

"I-I've grown a God-damn tail!" screamed Cynthia.

"M-me too," whimpered Heidi from the floor.

Then, Cynthia's arms and legs began twisting, bulging and stretching in impossible, painful ways. Yelping, she lost her balance and hit the floor with a thud. As she lay there, screaming in agony, her calves, feet, and thighs elongated, pushing her body along the floor, leathery pads forming on her soles. Her biceps twitched. They too began to swell, grotesquely thick veins pulsating along their length. The rest of her arms followed suit, widening, bulging with powerful muscles. Her back muscles arched up over her head. Her chest and stomach tightened as thick lines of sinew impressed themselves against her fur-lined skin.

A final spasm of growth tore the last shreds her clothing from her body. Now naked, Cynthia heard a wolf howl coming from the showers. She could also make out Heidi twitching and pounding against the floor beside her. Cynthia moaned, her voice steadily becoming more guttural and bass. Her face stretched out. Her nose darkened. Her ears traveled up her head and grew long and pointed. Her eyes began to glow red. Blood drooled from her lips as her teeth lengthened into razor-sharp fangs. The pain came to a mind-shattering crescendo as her jaw and nose pushed out in tandem, forming a muzzle. Overwhelmed, terrified, and trembling in agony, Cynthia raised her lupine head and howled, her ululation filling the locker room, drowning out all other sound. Her call was soon answered by Heidi, who raised her own head into the air and gave her pain voice. The twin howls hung in the air, and then slowly faded away.

From her hiding spot behind the cart Melinda slumped against the wall.

"Yikes," she breathed.

Despite everything she couldn't help but feel a little sorry for them. She remembered how terrifying it had been for her the first time - not to mention the excruciating pain.

Suddenly, a high-pitched beeping sound filled the air of the girls' locker room.

"Uhhh."

Melinda cursed softly as she shut off her watch's alarm, not bothering to check the time. She pressed her body up against the laundry cart and peered over it.

It was Heidi. Although she could make out very little of her body with the row of waist-high lockers in the way she could tell it was her by the russet fur. The red-headed cheerleader had woken up and was trying, unsuccessfully, to get to her feet. Melinda heard a sort of scrabbling sound – like a dog frantically scampering across a hard, slick surface. After nearly half-a-minute of this, Heidi lifted herself up. Wobbling unsteadily, she turned around so her back was up against the lockers, giving Melinda a clear view of her body.

She stood head to toe at a height of at least seven feet. She was covered in a thick layer of reddish-brown fur that lightened to a near red at her shoulders. The fur running down her chest and stomach, however, was light tan while her mane was nearly the same shade of red her hair had been before her transformation. Her head sported a partial muzzle, raised, pointed ears and a black snout – an amalgam of human and lupine features, like Melinda's – but underneath it all the face was unquestionably Heidi's; Melinda even swore she could make out little patches of darkened fur along her cheeks where her freckles had been – still quite attractive in an odd way. Her physique was as impressive as Melinda's – packed with powerful, toned muscles visible even under the mass of fur. To say she looked confused and disoriented would be a gross understatement.

A large shape suddenly rose into view from the lockers. Melinda nearly gasped in astonishment.

A *blonde* werewolf?

Cynthia's coat had in fact darkened into a light brown during her transformation but retained a yellowish hue, bringing Melinda more to mind of a golden retriever than a wolf. Her hair, however, had not changed much in color or length, remaining golden blonde. She had a very sleek, almost streamlined appearance, not too shaggy or too short, though still clearly powerfully built. Like Heidi, Melinda could see a bit of Cynthia's human features on her lupine face – smooth cheeks, dainty, ovoid chin, slightly pursed lips – all of which still looked gorgeous even though she was half-wolf. To her mild surprise, Melinda felt a familiar twinge of jealousy as she observed Cynthia; it didn't help that her new form was just as curvy as her human one.

Melinda shook her head, sighing, and tried to turn her attention back to the two cheerleaders, but found she was having trouble maintaining her concentration…

* * *

Cynthia shook her head in a daze. Her head felt as though it had been pounded with a mallet. Her vision was a gray blur.

"Rrrrr…Who…wh…Heidi?" she murmured vaguely, rubbing her forehead.

Cynthia blinked. She looked down at her hands. Four rotating yellow blobs gradually coalesced into two yellow, furry, talon-adorned paws. Her lower lip quivered as she ran them down her sides, feeling the alien sensation of fur rubbing against fur. She screamed, stepping back in panic only to slip and nearly fall back to the floor. As she struggled to regain her balance she collided with something. She whirled around. Standing before her was Heidi, who was nursing a bruised…tail?

"HEIDI!" screamed Cynthia.

"CYNTHIA!" screamed Heidi.

Not knowing what to do the two teenagers stood there in shock, their eyes rapidly scanning each others bodies in astonishment.

After what seemed to be an eternity, one of them spoke.

"RRRrrwhat the hell happened to you?" said Cynthia in terrified awe, cupping her mouth when she heard her new, deeper voice.

"…Well, what the hell happened to you?" replied Heidi nervously, her voice also noticeably deeper.

Both girls gulped and stared down at their bodies.

"What the fuck…?" murmured Cynthia as she rubbed the thick pads on her left paw.

Heidi whimpered as she looked down at her new tail. It tucked itself between her legs as though trying to avoid her gaze. Cynthia sniffed the air and sneezed violently as thousands of new odors overwhelmed her senses.

"Er…girls?" intoned a voice behind them.

Heidi and Cynthia yelped and spun around. Standing there before them was a gray-furred wolf-like creature much like them, though noticeably shorter and less muscular than either of the two. It was female - unmistakably female - with a long bushy tail, yellow eyes, tall, pointed ears and a muzzle.

"It's me! - Lily!" exclaimed the creature after a while.

Cynthia's jaw dropped.

"Oh God, you too?" she croaked.

"Yeah," muttered Lily wretchedly, wrapping her arms around her fur-covered body.

The three girls just stared at each other. Finally, Heidi spoke.

"W-wha-what are we going to do?"

"What are we?" whimpered Lily, staring down at her body.

"Jesus, look at us!" breathed Cynthia.

The formally silent locker room soon filled with the frantic babble of the three girls.

"How the hell did this happen?"

"I feel so weird!"

"What's that awful smell?"

"Oh God, I have claws!"

"Me too!"

"Hey," said an unfamiliar voice suddenly.

All three girls turned.

Standing there before them was yet another female wolf-creature. This one had jet-black fur and bright yellow eyes. The newcomer folded her thick arms and regarded the three dumbstruck cheerleaders with a toothy smirk.

"I told you that you were bitches," she said with overt satisfaction.

"Melinda!" gasped Cynthia.

"Yep," said Melinda happily.

"Y-you…you knew?"

"Knew what?" replied Melinda, her voice dripping with innocence.

"That we'd turn into these…these…just what the hell are we, anyway?" cried Cynthia.

Melinda rolled her yellow eyes.

"I told you. Bitches," she said.

"You *know* what I mean!" snarled Cynthia, angry.

"Fine, fine," said Melinda, savoring the moment. "You're werewolves."

"Werewolves?" breathed Heidi in astonishment.

"But there's no such thing," whimpered Lily pathetically.

Melinda shrugged.

"If you say so," she said.

"But....then…how?"

Melinda took a few steps forward, shaking her head.

"Well, it's a long story," she said. "But more immediately, it's because you chose the worst possible moment to torture a girl who has already been through hell and didn't need a bunch of stuck-up cheerleader sluts giving her grief."

Heidi and Lily looked at each other, confused, but Cynthia stared at Melinda in shock and realization.

"Yvette," she whispered.

"Yeah," said Melinda gravely.

"Wait, wait, wait," growled Cynthia, waving her paw. "She's a werewolf and…and you're a werewolf…just what the hell is going on here?" she roared.

"Calm down," said Melinda levelly. "I'll explain everything later. Right now we-"

"NO! Not later, NOW!" bellowed Cynthia, bearing her fangs. "What the FUCK is happening to us? You give us some goddamn answers now or I'll tear your throat out!"

Behind her, Heidi and Lily were backing away, unnerved by their leader's outburst. Melinda simply glared at Cynthia.

"I'm going to let that go because you're-"

"You and that little freak Yvette did this to us, didn't you?" snarled Cynthia, shoving Melinda. "Some kind of payback? This…this is fucking sick! You'd better change us back or I'll-"

Melinda roared and seized Cynthia by the shoulders, forcing her back. Cynthia struggled madly in her grasp until Melinda squeezed her so hard she yelped in pain. Melinda then slammed the terrified wolf-girl's head against the lockers. Heidi and Lily winced.

Melinda leaned over and whispered into Cynthia's ear.

"Don't…*ever* scream at me again," she said.

She let go. Cynthia fell limply to the floor. Her body had left a sizable dent in the metal locker door. She laid there for a few seconds, moaning, clutching her skull, and then scooted away and stood. Heidi, Lily, and Cynthia stood together in a quivering, frightened mass, staring at Melinda.

Melinda glared at them. "Listen," she growled. "We have to get out of here. It's only a matter of time before someone comes. Do you want to be caught looking like this?"

Three furry heads shook frantically.

"Then follow me."

Chapter 8

Escaping campus unnoticed proved to be much easier than Melinda had anticipated. There was one close encounter with the school janitor near the cafeteria, but Melinda shut off the hallway lights, leaving the man to fumble through the dark while the four of them hurried out the side exit. With Heidi, Lily, and Cynthia in tow she made her way out across the soccer field and into the wildlife preserve.

Melinda glanced back at the three cheerleaders-turned-werewolves. They were stumbling along in a daze, occasionally tripping over and walking on all fours for a couple yards before standing back up in a panic. None of them had uttered a word since the locker room.

"All right, we've gone far enough," announced Melinda. "We can stop."

The three girls nodded dumbly and lowered themselves to the ground. They shifted their legs and bodies awkwardly as they tried to find a sitting position comfortable for their altered physiology.

"Like this," said Melinda, crossing her legs then sliding them between each other as she sat. It had taken her a bit of practice to master the maneuver.

Heidi and Lily complied, managing the trick after a few false starts. Cynthia, however, was having trouble getting a hang of it. She bent her knees but then slipped to the dirt with a canine yelp then clumsily rolled over on all fours. Melinda rose with a sigh and approached her.

"Here, try-"

"Keep away from me!" whined Cynthia, backing away.

"Look, if you just turn over this way and-" continued Melinda.

"RRrr...No! Stay back!" cried Cynthia.

Melinda rubbed her forehead, growling in frustration. She was about to reprimand Cynthia when she noticed there were tears rolling down the cheerleader's furry yellow face.

Melinda stood there in stunned silence. She had never seen Cynthia cry before; indeed, show any emotion other than jealousy, anger, or cruel glee.

"Please, Cynthia, I'm just trying to help," said Melinda as kindly as she could manage.

"Shut up! Shut up! Shut up!" sobbed Cynthia, clutching her furry knees.

"I know you're scared, but-"

"Just leave me alone. You won, alright! I-I-I'm a monster. A freak. I'll...I'll have to live out in the forest or...or end up in some lab."

"M-Maybe our folks can help us out," said Heidi hopefully, looking up. "My dad could-"

"Listen, you're not stuck like this!" said Melinda urgently. "None of you are! Tomorrow morning you're going to change back."

"W-what?" said Cynthia, confused.

"Werewolves - only have to change during a full moon, remember?" said Melinda. "When the sun rises you'll be human again."

There was a long pause. Cynthia and Lily seemed to calm down a little, but Heidi glanced uneasily at Melinda.

"But...from now on we're going to change every full moon, right?" she asked sadly.

Melinda opened her mouth, hesitated for a second, and then nodded.

"Jesus," muttered Lily, her ears drooping.

Cynthia moaned and buried her head in her arms. Heidi stared down at the dirt, sulking. Melinda silently watched the three cheerleaders-turned-werewolves. She shook her head.

"Look, I know this is...really scary," began Melinda. "But you can't just sit here all night feeling sorry for yourselves."

"What the fuck are we supposed to do then, huh?" snapped Heidi.

Melinda glared at her but resisted the impulse to growl. Instead, she took a deep breath and continued.

"For starters, don't you want to know what's going on?" she asked.

Heidi blinked in surprise.

"Uh, yeah," she said hesitantly.

Melinda cleared her throat.

She told them how she had gotten lost while camping, how she had fallen into a sinkhole and been bitten by a strange beast. She recounted her first full moon night after the encounter, how she had transformed into the creature standing before them. She explained how the transformation had changed her, physically and mentally, and how she had adapted. The cheerleaders listened quietly, occasionally shaking their head or gasping in disbelief.

"It really isn't bad at all," insisted Melinda. "The biggest headache is scheduling everything around full moon nights. Otherwise…well, it's one of the best things that's ever happened to me."

"How can you say that?" exclaimed Cynthia in a frightened tone. "I mean…right now I…GOD!" she pounded the dirt. "I feel so fucked up. It's worse than the time I tried ecstasy."

"I know what you mean," growled Heidi. "Like being wasted and jacked up on caffeine at the same time. And my muscles still hurt like hell. "

"It takes some getting used to," said Melinda. "But it does get better. You three probably had it rougher than me since the change happened so suddenly."

Cynthia looked up at Melinda sharply.

"W-Wait a minute," she said. "Yvette…how did *she* become a werewolf? She's the one who bit us and turned us into these…these things."

Melinda winced. She had been hoping to avoid answering that particular question.

"You…you bit her, didn't you?" breathed Cynthia before Melinda had a chance to reply. "The night of the game against Asbury."

Frowning, Melinda nodded. All three girls gasped.

"Why would you…why would do that?" exclaimed Cynthia angrily, rising.

This time Melinda did growl in response. She marched over to Cynthia and glared at her, daring her to try something. For a moment Cynthia met her irate gaze with one of her own, but then the yellow-haired werewolf blinked and timidly backed away. Fury slowly drained from Melinda's face, leaving a pained expression. She turned away from the three cheerleaders, staring into the dark forest.

"I'm not proud of what I did," said Melinda. "Yvette caught me in the middle of transforming. I tried to explain but…she's really scared of wolves, so she ran. I chased her, tackled her, then she bit me while trying to escape so I…I…it just sort of happened. The next day…well, you saw what she was like." She turned back to the three girls and shot them a murderous look. "I was trying to help her through it when you showed up."

"How the fuck were we supposed to know she was turning into a werewolf?" exclaimed Heidi.

There was a pause.

"Fair enough," responded Melinda levelly. "But anyone with half a brain could have seen she was under a lot of stress and you pushed her over the edge. I mean, seriously, what is your problem with her?"

"What's our problem with her? What's her problem with *us*?" said Cynthia. "Why couldn't she take the hint and stay the fuck away from us?"

"Didn't you four used to be best friends or something?" probed Melinda.

"Well, yeah, back in the third grade," snorted Cynthia.

"So? What happened? Yvette never really explained why you broke up."

Cynthia made a noise somewhere between a snarl and a sigh, rubbing her furry forehead.

"Why are we discussing this, Melinda?" she said in an exasperated voice. "God, I mean…I just changed into a goddamn werewolf and al-"

"Answer the question!" barked Melinda.

"Fine!" snapped Cynthia. "We just…drifted apart, OK? We changed and she didn't. She's still the same, lame, little goody two-shoes she was when we were all still finger-painting. Not to mention that pretentious fake accent of hers. God, do you know how embarrassing it can be to be around her?"

"Maybe I do," said Melinda. "But you know what? She's still my friend and one of the nicest people you've ever met. Since when is being *nice* a bad thing? And by the way, she IS French, so yes, she has an accent."

All three girls were staring at her, mouths agape.

"But you know what?" continued Melinda, now on a roll. "Forget about all that for a second. I've never been too fond of the way you've treated me, either. Do you have any idea how many times you made me cry? Made me think about KILLING myself? I tried to warn you about this but you never gave me a chance."

"We were pissed," managed Cynthia. "Who wouldn't be? Especially after that…that trick you pulled at the cafeteria."

"And before that little incident?" asked Melinda sweetly. "Before I started standing up for myself?"

"We were…we were just having a little fun with you…" Cynthia's voice petered out.

There was silence.

"Yeah, fun," said Melinda emotionlessly.

The quiet sounds of the forest hung in the air.

"So…what happens now?" asked Heidi uncertainly.

Melinda turned back to the preserve. She gazed into the seemingly endless expanse of trees, absently sniffing the cool evening wind.

"I'm going to help you through this," said Melinda finally. "I'll teach you everything I've learned about being a werewolf." She turned. "And you're going to help me bring Yvette back," she added.

"Wait, what?"

"I'm the one who transformed her and you're the ones who drove her away," said Melinda steadily. "We're both responsible for what happened to her so we're both going to make it right."

"Forget it!" cried Cynthia. "Melinda…we need to…to go to the police or something or…or the FBI or CIA! Heidi? Heidi! What the fuck are you doing?"

While they were talking Heidi had stood up and wandered a couple feet away from the group. She was staring at the full moon.

"Ah!…sorry, what were you saying?" said Heidi, whirling around.

Melinda smiled knowingly before continuing. "Yvette is somewhere out there," she said, pointing a clawed digit. "Angry, scared, confused. Forget the fact you drove her away AND she could hurt someone. She needs help and she's a…a fellow human being. If you any shred of a conscience you'll help me find her."

"Why do you need our help anyways?"

"Because *she's* a werewolf too, remember? If she won't listen to reason we may have to restrain her and I'm not sure I could do it on my own. The more of us there are, the better the chance we can take her down without anyone getting hurt."

The three girls were silent.

"Come on!" said Melinda, wringing her paws. "You're stuck out here for the next night or two either way."

"Okay, okay," said Heidi, rising. "Let's…say we do help you. How the hell are we going to find her, huh? This preserve is huge!"

"Using these," Melinda said, tapping her nose. "In case you haven't noticed, werewolves have really good senses of smell. We just have to find her trail and follow it; it's less than a day old."

Lily frowned. She had been sitting in thoughtful silence the entire time.

"Well, I…I guess we could give you a hand," she murmured, rising.

"Lily!" cried Cynthia angrily.

"She has a point, Cynthia," snapped Lily with surprising fierceness, brushing dirt from her pelt.

"Besides, we might as well get used to this," said Heidi, gesturing at her body. "I don't like the little freak any more than you do, Cynthia, but I don't want her to get hurt."

To Cynthia's astonishment the two other cheerleaders turned werewolves walked past her and joined Melinda.

"So, uh, what's the plan?" said Heidi distractedly, glancing off into the woods.

"Hang on!" shouted Cynthia. "You two are actually going with her?"

Melinda gave Cynthia a hard look.

"You don't want to help?" she said. "Fine. Stay here and keep out of sight."

Melinda turned and walked away. Heidi and Lily glanced at Cynthia timidly, gave apologetic shrugs and then hurried off after her. Cynthia stood there, fuming.

"Don't you think our parents are going to miss us when we don't come home, huh?" she called. "What if she left the preserve? What if she's already dead? You three are insane! This whole fucking thing is insane!"

By the time she had finished her rant both Heidi and Lily had disappeared into the forest. Now alone, Cynthia looked around nervously, hugging her shoulders, shaking. Her nose twitched and she winced, clutching her muzzle.

"Damn it," she whispered, lowering her paw.

She scurried after them.

Midnight had come and gone. Dark clouds were rolling in from the north, dimming the stars and the moon. Every so often a cold wind would sweep through the forest, sending branches swaying and leaves rustling on the ground. Then the wind would die down and all would be silent again.

Melinda crouched low. She reached down and slowly ran her paw across the forest floor. She picked up a small clod of dirt and leaves and crumbled it, rubbing it between her black padded digits. She sighed.

"Anything?"

Melinda glanced over her shoulders. Heidi was standing a few feet away. To Melinda's keen vision her form was distinct but monochromatic save for her eyes, which glowed pale green.

"Not sure," said Melinda uncertainly. "Maybe Yvette. Could be a bit of sweat or hair. It's really faint."

She stood and strode back towards Heidi, wiping her paws.

"Damn it, we lost her trail," she hissed.

Heidi shrugged. Melinda looked past her over at Cynthia and Lily. The blonde werewolf was leaning against a tree, staring longingly back in the direction they had come. Lily was standing a couple yards away, eyes shut, sniffing.

"Hey, what are you two doing?" asked Melinda, addressing Cynthia.

"Don't ask me," said Cynthia sourly. "Ask Lily."

"Hey, can the attitude," said Melinda reproachfully, marching over to her. "I didn't make you come."

"Yeah, sure," muttered Cynthia. "Hey, Lily, what the hell are you doing?"

Lily opened her eyes.

"I…think I smell her," she whispered.

"What?" exclaimed Melinda and Cynthia.

"She's…" Lily shut her eyes again and inhaled deeply through her nose "…She's that way," she said, pointing a claw southeast.

Melinda raised her nose, breathing in the myriad scents around her. Pine bark, dead leaves, mildew, raccoon urine, engine fumes, the musk of Cynthia, Heidi, and Lily, bird droppings, pinecones, pollen…

…And a very faint but very familiar aroma.

"It is her," gasped Melinda. She turned to Lily. "How did you pick it up?" she said in amazement.

Lily shrugged nervously.

"I don't know," she said. "I mean, when I first…you know, changed, everything just got really smelly. I could barely breathe through my nose. But now it's much…clearer."

Melinda stared at Lily.

"Are you sure?" said Heidi, stepping forward. She sniffed. "I can't smell her."

"It's really faint and it helps if you already know what she smells like," said Melinda absently.

"Huh, that's pretty cool, Lily," said Heidi, grinning. "Way to go."

Lily smiled. From beneath her tree, Cynthia rolled her eyes.

"Come on, let's go," exclaimed Melinda.

Melinda fell to all fours and scurried in the direction of Yvette's scent. She had gone a couple hundred yards when she realized the other girls were lagging behind her. She stopped, peered back at them, and immediately saw the problem.

"Stop running like that!" she yelled.

"What?"

"Get down and run like a wolf," called Melinda. "You move a lot faster."

"You're kidding, right?"

"Just try it!"

Melinda turned and continued running.

A minute or so later Heidi suddenly appeared alongside her, furiously sprinting on all fours just as she had suggested. Melinda did a double take.

"Hi 'Linda!" she barked, grinning manically.

Smirking, Melinda accelerated, darting nimbly between the trees and bushes, quickly outpacing Heidi.

"Hey! Slow down," cried Heidi.

Suddenly, Yvette's scent grew stronger. Melinda slowed to a canter. Heidi shot past her and disappeared into the woods. A few seconds later she circled back and reappeared.

"Awww, tired already?" laughed Heidi, playfully bounding sideways.

"Slow down," growled Melinda, trying to focus on the scent. "She's close."

Soon Lily and Cynthia appeared from behind, Lily trotting on four legs and Cynthia stubbornly jogging on two.

Melinda began combing the area, searching for any sign of Yvette.

"Wait, Melinda!" cried Lily suddenly.

Melinda, Heidi, and Cynthia stopped and turned. Lily was crouching next to a cypress in a small clearing.

"You're going to want to see this," said Lily nervously.

A lump formed in Melinda's throat. She trotted over to Lily and peered down at the ground.

Before she saw what was lying there she caught a whiff of Yvette's scent. It was strong. It wasn't just the smell of sweat, skin and tears, either; there was blood. When she gazed down she realized why.

Shreds of dirty fabric were strewn across the grass. Melinda crouched down to get a better look. Although she couldn't identify the colors in the dim light she recognized the material. She reached down and picked up a tiny fragment and smelled it.

"It's Yvette's," she whispered

Her gaze traveled across the ground and up the cypress. Long, deep claw marks had been gouged in its trunk.

"This is where it happened," said Melinda, slightly louder. "This is where she transformed."

Grim silence followed.

"How the hell did she get this far on foot?" whispered Heidi.

"We're not that far from the school," said Cynthia. "We've been moving along the perimeter of the forest, remember?"

Suddenly, Lily stepped forward, sniffing the air.

"Oh Christ, now what, Lily?" exclaimed Cynthia. "Timmy fell down a well?"

There was a menacing growl. Cynthia froze and slowly turned to Melinda, who was suddenly inches away from her face.

"Keep pushing it," spat Melinda, fangs flashing in the dim light. "See what happens."

"W-What?" said Cynthia with a strange mixture of defiance, bluster and fear. "You're going to kill me just for making a joke?"

"You are unbelievable, you know that?" exclaimed Melinda. "Don't you get it? She could get killed if we don't find her. Or she could kill someone else."

"You don't know that," protested Cynthia. "Maybe she's just lost, or something."

"One, if she's a werewolf there's no way she'd get lost. Two, there's something seriously wrong with her. You saw the state she was in." Melinda stared into the forest. "She's reacting differently to the transformation, I know it. She needs our help."

"No, she needs YOUR help," retorted Cynthia. "You're the one who bit her; you're the one who pissed her off. You take care of it!"

"Would you two give it a rest?" interrupted Heidi. "For Christsakes, Cynthia, it's not that bad."

Cynthia whirled around.

"Whose side are you on, Heidi?" she snapped angrily.

"I'm not on anyone's side!" exclaimed Heidi. "Who cares about sides anymore, huh? Things have kind of changed! WE'VE changed. Even if Yvette is as annoying as hell we at least owe her this, don't we?"

Cynthia stared at Heidi in shock. Her eyes narrowed into slits of rage. Chest swelling, nostrils flaring, she opened her mouth to speak and then, like a balloon that had suddenly lost all its air, deflated. Saying nothing, she hung her head and turned away, tail tucked between her legs.

Surprised but grateful, Melinda nodded at Heidi. She then glanced over at Lily, who had been sniffing the air as though nothing had happened.

"It's not just her," muttered Lily. "I smell…" she licked her lips "Meat, blood, fat…"

Melinda stared at her, wide-eyed.

"It's…a deer," said Lily, reading her expression. "I think it's a deer, anyways. Not human, at least," she added.

Melinda breathed a sigh of relief.

"She must have caught it right after changing," said Melinda. "You always get hungry after…"

She trailed off, staring blankly into space. Then, she chuckled, shaking her head. Heidi, Lily, and even Cynthia looked at her in confusion.

"No wonder you all are so tense," she laughed. "No wonder I'm so tense. We're hungry."

As if to punctuate the observation, someone's stomach rumbled.

"Now that you mention it, yeah, I'm starving," said Lily uneasily.

"Yeah," said Heidi. "I was…well, too scared to say anything before."

"We don't have a chance of catching up with Yvette if she's eaten and we haven't," said Melinda. "We need some food."

"Yeah, but, where are we going to go?" asked Heidi. "It's not like we can stop by the 7/11 or anything."

"I guess we'll hunt for our dinner too," sighed Melinda. "Damn, it's still going to cost us some time."

This drew horrified gasps from the three girls.

"*Hunt?*" exclaimed Lily. "As in…hunt deer and bunnies and stuff?"

"We're werewolves, remember?" said Melinda dryly.

"Yeah, but we're not actually going to...to chase down and kill some poor animal, are we?" whimpered Heidi.

"What's the big deal?" said Melinda, taking perverse pleasure in their discomfort. "I heard you once went hunting with your dad."

"That's different," protested Heidi. "We just shot the damn things. We didn't...ewww!"

Melinda grinned wickedly.

"You say that," she said mischievously. "But right now, I bet you can't stop thinking about a big, thick, tender, juicy, red steak, dripping with warm, glistening blood."

She noted with some satisfaction the flicker of hunger in their eyes. Then, Cynthia shuddered.

"No way, just...no way," she said shaking her head. "That's just gross. Not happening."

* * *

The deer lowered its head to the grass. It briefly nuzzled the thick assemblage of blades - sniffing them - then started chewing. Every so often it would raise its head to scan its surroundings and then return to its meal. A light breeze passed through the forest. Its head immediately shot up. It backed away a few feet, nervously pawing at the wet ground. A full minute passed - nothing happened. The gentle creature hesitantly returned to the grass and continued to feed.

A low-throated growl emerged from the surrounding woods. The deer froze.

A huge, brown beast leapt from bushes in an explosion of leaves and dirt. It scampered wildly towards the frightened creature, howling as it ran. The deer was off in a flash. It bounded and leapt through the thick undergrowth. It had gotten no farther than a dozen yards when a second beast - this one dark grey - charged in from the deer's right. The terrified animal frantically arced to the left to avoid the newcomer, nearly colliding with a tree. The two creatures were soon in hot pursuit. Yet despite their frenzied effort the deer was gaining ground. Though fast, the two beasts were as not as agile as their prey. It slid smoothly between trees and bushes while the two lumbering creatures savagely tore through the foliage.

All of a sudden two large shapes leapt out from behind the trees ahead of the deer. The doe bleated in surprise as one of the shapes tackled it. It thrashed frantically on the ground for a second but then a powerful set of jaws gripped its neck and squeezed. There was a snap. The deer's body went limp.

Melinda spat the neck out and licked the blood from her mouth. Heidi and Lily trotted up besides her and Cynthia. The doe lay there before them - unmoving. The four werewolves silently regarded the body.

Melinda glanced at her three companions, and then sighed.

"It's okay," she said quietly.

Without another moment's hesitation, claws unsheathed, the four werewolves tore into the deer.

* * *

Melinda found Cynthia sitting on a fallen tree gazing up at the starry night sky. The clouds above had thinned enough to permit a trickle of moonlight to shine down upon them; Cynthia's flaxen pelt seemed to glow in the gentle illumination.

"Hey, Cynthia," said Melinda softly.

At first Cynthia did not turn or indeed react in any obvious fashion. She just sat there. Then, she glanced over her shoulder and nodded.

"We need to get going," said Melinda. "It's got to be three hours past midnight. The longer we wait the harder it will be to catch up with Yvette."

Cynthia sighed deeply. She slowly rose, turned, and approached Melinda.

"How do you do it?" asked Cynthia.

"What do you mean?" said Melinda, cocking her head.

Cynthia's expression was that of tired awe tinged with bitterness.

"Carry on like this," she said, gesturing at the forest. "Christ, Melinda, how can you…how did you get up and go to school every day after this?"

Melinda was silent.

"I'm not saying it's bad," added Cynthia thoughtfully. "Just really weird and creepy. Part of me wishes this never happened and another part…" she shivered "…another part wants to run into the forest and never come out."

Melinda shrugged diffidently.

"I don't know, Cynthia," she said wearily. "It happened, and I adapted as best I could. It wasn't perfect. I guess you could say I made it work. Now come on."

Cynthia glared at her.

"Whatever," she said, waving a paw.

She took a few steps past her and then stopped suddenly and turned her head.

"You ever consider what's going to happen after you graduate?" she asked suspiciously. "What'll you do after college? What'll happen if you fall in love or just want to fool around with some guy? What'll happen if our little secret gets out?"

Melinda blinked.

"Uh, um…" she murmured, nonplussed.

"Um, yeah. Glad to see you worked everything out," remarked Cynthia sardonically. "So, you coming?"

Lost in thought, Melinda looked up in surprise.

"Yeah," she said uncertainly.

The two werewolves made their way through the trees.

Chapter 9

Lily froze and began sniffing. Behind her, Heidi, Cynthia, and Melinda stopped in their tracks and waited for her to finish.

"Why is she so good at this?" whispered Heidi to Melinda.

"No clue," said Melinda. "Did she always have such a good sense of smell?"

"Not that I've ever noticed," said Heidi. "Cynthia?"

"No," said Cynthia, eying Lily.

"I can hear you, you know," said Lily without turning around.

The three werewolves looked at her in surprise and then mild embarrassment.

"Her scent just got stronger," continued Lily after a while. "She's…just ahead, I think."

Melinda's heart leapt. She took a deep breath and sure enough, there was Yvette's musk. She broke into a run, disappearing into a thick clump of trees. The other wolf-girls hesitated and then followed her. When they caught up with her she was standing on her hind-legs on top of a rocky ledge, staring out into the night. Heidi and Lily nearly tumbled over the precipice in their haste.

"Yikes," yelped Heidi, stepping back.

A few dislodged pebbles fell down the cliff.

Melinda nodded, gazing downward. Below was a narrow, wooded valley. It looked as though it was at least a hundred feet to the bottom. Her ears twitched. She heard the trickle of running water. She narrowed her eyes and saw a thin, telltale glitter of a stream snaking between the two rock faces.

"Didn't know this was out here," whispered Heidi.

"I think we've left the nature preserve," said Melinda vaguely. "The forest goes on for about five more miles and then…" she gulped. "Then it hits the freeway."

As Melinda scanned the dale, searching for some egress into it or way around it, something caught her attention.

"Hang on," said Melinda, raising paw.

"What?"

Melinda narrowed her eyes. The distance and thick foliage below conspired against her vision. She wasn't quite sure what it is she had seen – not so much a color or a silhouette as much a flash of motion near the water.

"There it is again!' exclaimed Melinda.

"I saw it too," whispered Lily.

There was something moving at the bank of the river. Something big.

"You…think it's Yvette?" said Heidi uncertainly.

"Maybe," said Melinda, staring at the distant figure. She sniffed. "Her smell is definitely coming from below."

Heidi leaned forward and smelled the air.

"Yeah, you're right," she said excitedly.

To Melinda's horror the auburn werewolf stood up on her hind-legs and called out.

"YVETTE! UP HERE!" she cried, waving a paw.

"No!" yelled Melinda angrily, pulling her down.

Lily and Cynthia quickly piled on.

"Hey, HEY! The fuck?" protested Heidi as she was dragged to the ground.

"Think about it, dumb ass," hissed Cynthia into her ear. "We're not exactly her favorite people in the world right now."

"Look!" cried Lily, pointing.

Melinda's eyes widened. A lone figure was running across the valley towards the opposite end – on four legs. It was large and white.

"Shit," breathed Melinda.

She scrambled to her feet. She looked to her right and her left desperately searching for some path down into the valley but all she saw was sheer cliff.

"Think, think, there's gotta be a way down," she murmured to herself.

Her mind raced. If they just jumped they could probably survive the fall, but she didn't know how long it would take them to recover. By the time they healed Yvette could be long gone.

"We'll have to go around," groaned Lily.

"It's too far," snarled Melinda. "We'll lose her."

Cynthia stepped forward, looking thoughtful. She glanced down the crag, bent over, and ran her paw along the side.

"What are you doing, Cynthia?" said Heidi, confused.

Cynthia flexed her wrist. Sharp, black talons emerged from her digits.

"Here's an idea," she muttered.

Still squatting, the blonde werewolf spun around so her back was to the valley. She carefully lowered herself over the ledge until she was hanging off the side.

Melinda turned and saw what Cynthia was doing.

"What in the-"

Cynthia disappeared over the edge.

"CYNTHIA!" screamed Melinda.

Melinda, Heidi, and Lily rushed over to the ledge and peered down. To their astonishment they saw Cynthia still clinging to the side, sliding down into the valley. They saw her glance up at them and grin smugly before vanishing into the darkness below.

"How did she...?" said Heidi, confused.

"Her claws," breathed Melinda.

Melinda bent over and vaulted over the edge. She twisted around and dug her claws and feet into the ledge. To her mild surprise the surface proved fairly yielding. Taking a deep breath, she lurched back.

Melinda yelped as she plunged downwards. Vertigo gripped her. For a moment she thought she had lost her hold and was falling uncontrollably into the valley. Then, she felt a tug as the cliff curved inward, drawing her along the rock face. Gritting her teeth, she pressed her feet deeper into the side, slowing her descent. Melinda winced. It felt as though her claws were being torn out of their sheaths but she didn't dare let go.

She risked a glance downwards and saw she was only ten feet from the bottom. She sighed in relief and, a few seconds later, dropped to the ground.

As she massaged her aching paws her ears twitched. She looked upwards and saw Heidi and Lily sliding down the cliff. The two werewolves eventually touched bottom; Lily didn't let go until her legs hit the ground, causing her to tumble over.

"That...was...awesome!" exclaimed Heidi, grinning wildly.

"Speak for yourself," growled Lily, staggering to her feet.

Despite the urgency of the situation Melinda could not help but chuckle. Then, the wind shifted. Melinda whirled around, sniffing the air.

"Yvette," she whispered.

"SHE'S OVER HERE!"

The voice had been Cynthia's. Melinda peered through the woods and spied Cynthia on the other side of the narrow river, waving her paws.

"C'MON! C'MON!" called Cynthia frantically.

Melinda needed no further prompting. She fell to all fours and scampered through the thick foliage. She slowed as she approached the river, but then noticed there were rocks sticking out in the center of the stream.

"IT'S ONLY A FOOT OR TWO AT IT'S DEEPEST!" yelled Cynthia.

Melinda sped up, dashing across the stream. The water was shockingly cold but Melinda quickly cleared the river's breadth, leaping across the raised piles of rocks until she reached the opposite shore. She shook the water from her fur and joined Cynthia.

"This way," said Cynthia anxiously.

Melinda followed her through the valley. Yvette's scent grew steadily stronger.

"I got a look at her," cried Cynthia as they ran.

"Yeah?"

"She…turned out different."

"What do you mean?" yelled Melinda.

Suddenly the forest opened up. Ahead was a small clearing at the base of the cliff. Melinda's eyes widened.

A monstrous beast was standing in the middle of the glade. The newcomer was enormous; standing on four legs it was nearly the size of a small sedan. It had a sleek, featureless white pelt and two amethyst eyes that glittered like the heart of winter. Its lips curled back, revealing rows of massive, razor-sharp ivory teeth set in blood-red gums.

"No," whimpered Melinda in disbelief. "It can't be…"

But one quick sniff confirmed the creature's identity.

The white wolf snarled angrily. She pawed at the ground like an enraged bull, looking ready to tear them to shreds.

"Yvette…it's me, remember?" said Melinda fearfully, raising her paws. "I know you're confused and angry but-"

The beast roared so loud Melinda and Cynthia were forced to cover their ears.

"I don't think she's in the mood to talk," muttered Cynthia, wincing.

The blonde werewolf stared at Yvette for a few seconds. Then, she charged.

"NO! Cynthia!" cried Melinda.

Caught off guard by Cynthia's unexpected move, the beast reared back in surprise. Cynthia darted nimbly from side-to-side and then pounced. She clung to the creature's right flank, crawled up along her body and grabbed her by the neck, putting her in a headlock. The beast bellowed furiously.

"Give me a hand here!" barked Cynthia as the great white wolf struggled in her grasp.

Melinda just stood there, mouth agape.

"SNAP OUT OF IT!" cried Cynthia.

Suddenly, the beast fell to the ground. Before Cynthia could react she rolled over on her back, crushing her under her ponderous weight.

"No!" cried Melinda.

The beast stood. Cynthia lay there on the ground, groaning. Before she could recover the white wolf tore into her. Cynthia screeched in pain as the massive werewolf tossed against a tree like a rag doll.

Melinda watched on in horror. Then, the smell of blood broke her trance. She hurried over to Cynthia and gasped at what she saw. Her stomach had been ripped open. Bloody entrails dangled grotesquely from her torso. Her fur was soaked in blood.

"That…bitch…" hissed Cynthia, clutching her wounded side.

Melinda fought back the urge to vomit. The sight of Cynthia's wound and the overwhelming scent of blood was making her gut churn.

Suddenly, she remembered Yvette. She looked up half-expecting to see the beast bearing down on her.

Instead, she saw nothing. No sign of Yvette. Nothing.

When she looked back down she was met with a bizarre sight. Cynthia's intestines were slowly crawling back into her. Her wound was closing, inch by inch.

"I knew we healed fast, but damn," breathed Melinda with equal parts wonder and disgust.

She heard padded footsteps behind her. She looked back and saw Heidi and Lily running towards them.

"Holy shit!" gasped Heidi, covering her mouth as she saw Cynthia.

"Is she-" whimpered Lily.

"She'll be OK,' said Melinda, rising. "Stay here and watch her until she gets back on her feet. I'll try to slow Yvette down until we can all catch up with her."

Melinda turned to leave.

"Wait!" croaked Cynthia, raising a paw.

Melinda stopped.

"You saw what she did to me," said Cynthia hoarsely. "Don't try to take her out yourself."

Melinda nodded slowly, and then disappeared into the woods.

* * *

"YVETTE!"

Melinda shot through the forest like a bat out of hell, utterly focused on the white wolf ahead of her.

"YVETTE!"

Again and again she called her friend's name to no response.

"COME BACK!"

Melinda howled in frustration and accelerated. The woods became a green blur. Sharp branches tore at her furry flank but she was far too high on adrenaline and desperation to notice or care.

"YVETTE!"

She was getting closer. She could see Yvette' long white tail.

"YVETTE!"

Suddenly, the great white wolf stopped dead in its tracks. Melinda yelped and skittered to a halt, stopping five feet from her quarry. She looked up and saw Yvette' snarling, monstrous visage staring down at her. Melinda eyes met hers. She did not see any sign of her friend behind those soulless, icy purple orbs.

Without warning the beast charged. Melinda instinctively dove to the side, barely evading the attack. She crouched low and sprang into the air, landing on Yvette' side. She clawed at Yvette thick fur and bit her ears. Yvette roared in surprise and pain. She shook angrily, bucking up and down, but could not dislodge Melinda. Suddenly, Yvette rushed forward and slammed her body into the moss-covered trunk of a towering evergreen. Melinda was thrown to the ground. She quickly scrambled to her feet but was knocked down by a vicious backhand paw-swipe. Before she could recover Melinda felt a crushing weight press down upon her. When she opened her eyes she found that Yvette had her pinned to the ground. She struggled to escape but found she could not move an inch. Yvette utterly overpowered her.

Melinda quivered in mortal terror as her former friend stared down at her.

"Yvette…please…it's me…Melinda…," whimpered Melinda.

The great white beast growled

"Remember…remember when…we went to the carnival in Branson? You…you got so sick on corn-dogs you threw up on the Merry-Go-Round."

The monster opened its massive jaws, preparing to rip Melinda apart.

It's no use, though Melinda bitterly. *She's all emotion now, and the only thing she remembers is how much she hates me.*

If only…

Melinda gulped as an idea came to her.

She shut her eyes and concentrated. Her instincts screamed in protest, rebelling against her seemingly suicidal impulse. Her entire body shook with effort. Using every ounce of willpower she possessed she overruled her urges and reflexes. Her fur receded. Her muscles shrank. Her tail crawled back into her body. Her muzzle flattened into a pink nose. The yellow light in her eyes flickered and died, replaced by two emerald motes.

Melinda lay there, naked and helpless. Her body was heavy with fatigue. Her muscles and bones were battered and sore. The night air chilled her pale pink flesh.

Yvette stared down in confusion.

"Yvette," said Melinda softly. "I'm sorry."

The harsh glare in Yvette' blue eyes softened.

"I'm so sorry," said Melinda, tears streaming down her cheek. "I just…I don't know. I was selfish and stupid and wanted to fit in. I've always taken our friendship for granted, and when I finally started to find other friends I just…tossed you aside. It was worst thing I've ever done to anybody. I wish I could take it back. You're the best friend anyone could hope for."

"I'm sorry," she sobbed. "I'm so sorry."

Melinda felt the weight over her lessen. Sniffling, she gazed upwards. Tears were budding in Yvette's own amethyst eyes.

Suddenly, Yvette lunged. Melinda screamed, thinking she was about to be devoured. Instead of a grisly death she felt a pair of strong arms embrace her. Yvette made a strange, guttural sound. It was not aggressive or threatening at all.

"S-sr-sr-sooorrry," intoned Yvette.

Melinda cried out in joy. She reached out and hugged Yvette, who lowered her body to the ground.

"Thank God," said Melinda. "I thought we'd lost you."

"S-ssooorrry," repeated Yvette, crying.

"Don't say you're sorry," said Melinda firmly. "Don't apologize for anything. Nothing that happened tonight was really your fault."

Melinda slipped out from under Yvette's arms and stared at the white-furred werewolf. She was quite different from herself and the cheerleaders – far more wolf-like. But now there was now a spark of intelligence and kindness in her eyes no mere beast could ever possess.

"You...turned out a bit differently from the rest of us," said Melinda in awe.

Suddenly, Yvette's head turned sharply. She growled.

"Hey."

Melinda looked in the direction Yvette had turned. Cynthia, Heidi, and Lily were standing a couple yards away. Apart from the blood on her chest it looked like Cynthia had recovered.

"Easy, Yvette," whispered Melinda nervously.

Cynthia stepped forward and sighed, shaking her head. After a few false starts, she spoke.

"Look I'm...sorry for all the shit I said about you, okay?" she said in a tone suggesting that, while genuinely remorseful, she was greatly annoyed at having admit it. "If you want to hang out with us I guess I wouldn't have a problem with it. Just...dial it down a bit, all right?" she added in a slightly friendlier voice.

Yvette yelped with joy, leapt to her feet and padded over to Cynthia, who stepped back nervously. The great white werewolf stood clumsily on two legs and gave Cynthia a massive hug and – to the laughter of everyone – started licking her.

"Hey! Jeez, I said dial it down, remember?" protested Cynthia, pushing Yvette away.

Yvette eventually backed away with a disappointed whine.

"We're, uh, we're sorry too," said Lily.

"Yeah," said Heidi, hanging her head.

Yvette nodded, and then turned sheepishly to Cynthia.

"S-S-Srroooorrry," she droned.

Cynthia looked at Yvette curiously.

"Can't you...talk?" she asked.

Yvette hesitated, and then shook her mane.

"...Hhhaaa...Haarrrrd...harrrrd," she managed.

"Must be the way your throat is shaped," said Melinda. "God, just when I think I'm starting to understand how this works..."

"Look, whatever," said Cynthia dismissively. "We found Yvette; you're fine, she's fine. Sort of. Everyone's happy." She pointed a thumb behind her. "Let's get the hell out of here."

Melinda smiled.

"That's the best idea I've heard all night," she said, standing.

Yvette walked over to Melinda, who nodded at her. Melinda shivered suddenly, clutching her shoulders.

"Well...before we go," said Melinda.

"What now?" groaned Cynthia.

"Could you get me some clothes?"

* * *

When morning came the sun crested the horizon, painting the sky a brilliant shade of orange. A lone howl pierced the air, soon followed by a second, then a third, a fourth, and a fifth. The chorus of voices filled the forest with their jubilant cadence, and then fell silent.

About The Lycanthrope Club

The Lycanthrope Club began an exercise in writing.

Years back when I was still an undergrad I was running an online roleplaying game called Grey on the Megatokyo forums. Grey was a complex thriller incorporating themes of transformation, duality, Jungian psychology and gnostic mythology. At its peak Grey was one of the most popular threads on the forums. However, I found myself drifting away from it. Collaborative work can be fun, but I wanted more control over the story. I wanted to write a full-length novella or novel.

I had been reading a lot of werewolf webcomics and fiction at the time. I was particularly impressed with Lobo Leo's *Alpha Luna* and the works of several authors at werewolf-themed Yahoo! Clubs. About half of the stories were, admittedly, fetish fodder, but the more I read the more I saw the werewolf as a spiritual successor to Grey – a creature caught between light and dark, man and animal, trying to reconcile its two halves to create a better whole. This has very little to do with the traditional werewolf of legend, but if vampires can be reinvented as sparkling, angst-ridden teen models then werewolves can certainly be more than slavering, bloodthirsty monsters.

This wasn't an original idea. Many other writers and artists had already depicted werewolves in a more positive (or at least different) light. However, there was one story I desperately wanted to read but never found: A female protagonist transforms into a werewolf and has to learn to live as one. She isn't cursed. She isn't blessed. She isn't the destined one. There is no secret society of werewolves and/or supernatural creatures for her to join or oppose. The story is about how she deals with such a profound and absurd transformation. On the face of it such a set-up lacks obvious conflict, but I like stories where there isn't a defined "good guy" and "bad guy" – where the plot flows from the situation. As for why I wanted a female protagonist, I could write an entire essay on the topic, but someone already has – "Hairy, thuggish women, female werewolves, gender, and the hoped-for monster," by Elizabeth M. Clark. In brief, contemporary culture regards female werewolves as disgusting because they clash with traditional gender values (hair and muscles associated with masculinity, gentleness and sweetness associated with femininity, etc.) yet there is potential in a "hopeful werewolf" figure who embraces her nature yet doesn't lose herself to her bestial side.

Eventually, I decided the only way I would get to read such a story would be to write it myself.

I initially viewed it more as an opportunity to improve my writing skills than a long term project. I wanted to improve my descriptive prose, and transformation scenes can be tricky. One has to balance detail with pacing, conveying the experience of the subject without getting bogged down. However, as I wrote the story I was surprised at how quickly and naturally it came together. When I posted the first chapter the response was extremely positive. To be fair, it was almost exclusively read by werewolf enthusiasts so there was definitely some audience bias. Still, the feedback was encouraging so I kept at it. The rest, as they say, is history. I finished the first novella and went on to write two more as well as several short stories set in the same universe. I started receiving fan-art from the very artists who inspired me in the first place.

Which brings us here, nearly a decade later, with the first book of what will hopefully be a trilogy. I was a little surprised at how how much editing it needed. I guess you could either say I've greatly improved as a writer or my early writing wasn't nearly as good as I thought it was. I also made significant changes to the plot, removing or changing elements I thought were weak. It took months of work, but I think the overall story is much stronger now.

I'd like to thank Kris Overstreet for editing the prologue and chapters 1 and 2, Lance Marcum for doing the final read-through and edit, Leo and Dirk for their excellent illustrations, and all of my readers for their continued support.

Tristan Eifler

Production Sketches

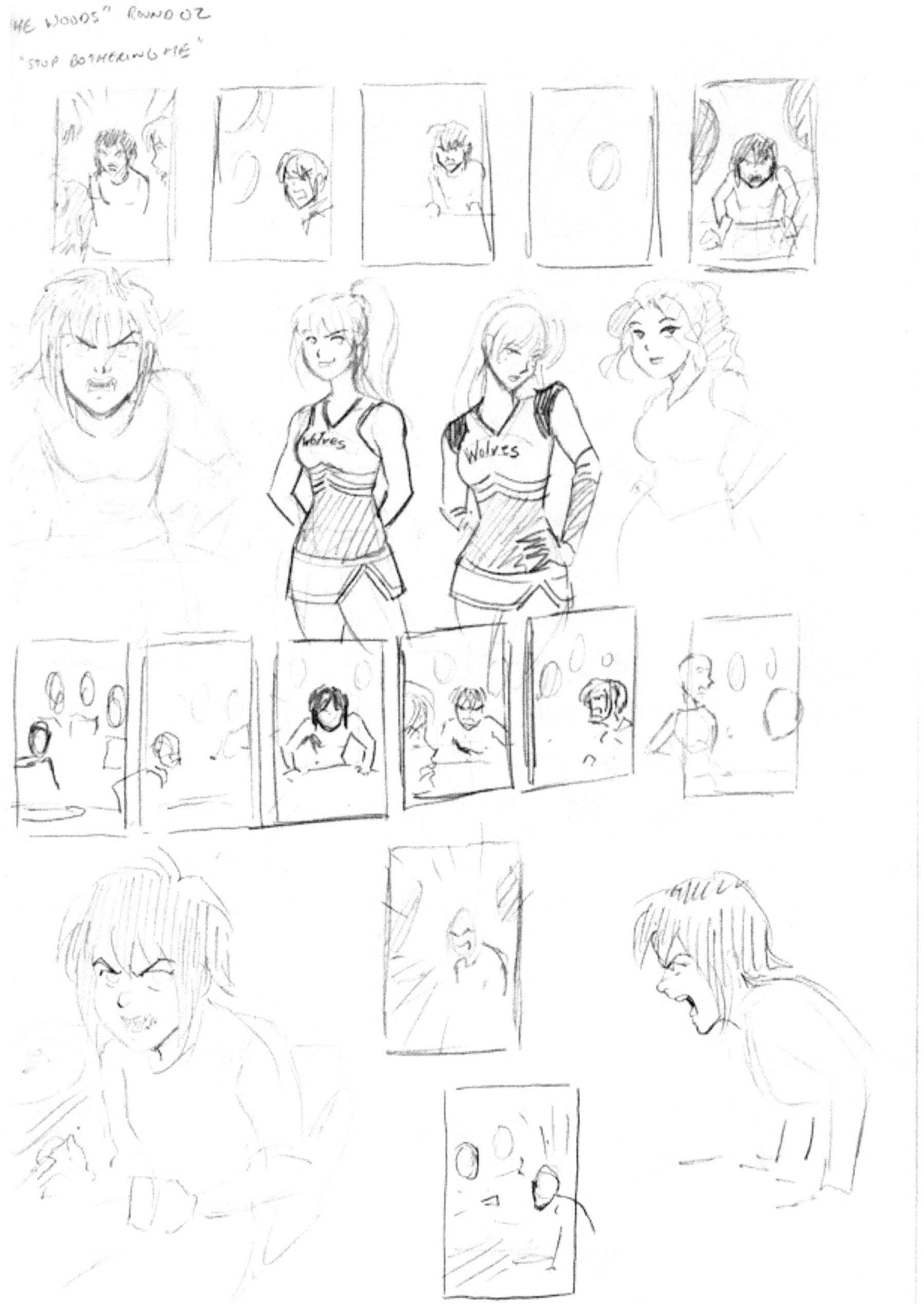
HE WOODS" ROUND 02
"STOP BOTHERING ME"
Wolves
Wolves

www.ingramcontent.com/pod-product-compliance
Lightning Source LLC
Chambersburg PA
CBHW08081725026
47159CB00010B/3421